About tl

I am the youngest of five sisters. Since I was a child, I've always had a vivid imagination and I entertained myself writing poetry, short novels, and even songs, as I do come from a very musical family. I guess writing, for me, was a quiet escape to lose myself in a fantasy world, especially from a household that was often hectic with four other siblings. I don't feel I had any special gift, but writing was literally like acting out a movie in my head and I could play all of the characters, which can be exhausting! I was born and raised in a small village in East Anglia. My mother and father both worked hard — neither would quit at any project no matter how difficult. My father would often say "There's no such word as 'can't'," and my mother's favourite words were, "Be determined, if you want something in life badly enough, always follow your dreams."

My other passion in life was to be a famous ballerina, and I studied ballet for several years, as well as the piano, and ballroom dancing. I have travelled throughout my life and love to experience new people and cultures. I have two adult children, one boy and one girl, who are both my heart, and I am now fortunate enough to have my first grandchild, who inspires me every day.

RABBIT RUNS

ESTELLE DALY ELLIS

RABBIT RUNS

Vanguard Press

VANGUARD PAPERBACK

© Copyright 2022
Estelle Daly Ellis

A CIP catalogue record for this title is
available from the British Library.

ISBN 978 1 80016 214 3

*Vanguard Press is an imprint of
Pegasus Elliot MacKenzie Publishers Ltd.*
www.pegasuspublishers.com

First Published in 2022

**Vanguard Press
Sheraton House Castle Park
Cambridge England**

Printed & Bound in Great Britain

Dedication

To my father, who has recently passed but always encouraged me to take my writing more seriously. I know he would have been very proud to see one of my manuscripts published.

To my mother, who has always shown dogged determination and has always succeeded in reaching her goals and her dreams.

To my beautiful children and my family.

To my friends on whom characters in this story are based, and who have been my rock in times of despair.

To my 'special friend', Soraya, who took the time to read the draft and inspired me with her kind and encouraging review to pursue a publisher and a career in writing.

A special dedication to my daughter who has been part of this process and tolerated my limited technical knowledge, and everyone who has encouraged me and supported me on this journey.

I would like to thank Pegasus Publishers who have given me this opportunity to pursue a career that I love and am very passionate about. Acknowledgement from such a reputable publisher has given me the confidence I needed and I am most grateful.

Finally, I would like to thank the character Darius, who supported me through the many storms and who has always been there. My prayers are with you now. Thank you and God bless.

1

Channelize was so excited to finally have the keys to their new apartment. She had been waiting forever to move away from Spain's prying eyes and wagging tongues. Hopefully, she could feel like herself again. The best feeling about the move was that no one knew anything about her and Darius, or their personal lives. As she opened the door, she sighed with relief. The apartment was exactly the way she had remembered it on her first visit, one month ago. The only difference was, that the debris from the previous tenants had been tidied away, which made the apartment look and feel even more appealing.

One of the most amazing features of the living room was the dominance of the large French windows, which she adored. They reminded her of a street scene from an old Oliver Twist movie. They looked out onto long cobbled alleyways occupied with pastry shops, antique and book shops, and overlooked terracotta slated roof tops. The church bells sounded every hour, on the hour. The ambiance was so typically French, thought Channelize. The main living area was spacious and airy. However, Channelize knew that she would change some of the decoration and put her own stamp on the place. The two-seater sofas were covered with large patterned throws in pink, orange and reds, which added an exuberance and warm, North African feel. Overall, it was very pretty and bright. There were several ornamental pieces, particularly a Moroccan-style brass jug, which was surrounded by four small goblets. Channelize assumed they were used for drinking mint tea, which was a local custom in Morocco. It was obviously a culture that Sarah, the landlady, had a fondness for. Channelize decided she would display this piece, as it was rather unusual.

She was suddenly jolted out of her thoughts by a figure hidden behind a pile of brown cardboard, crashing through the door, "Going to give me a hand with these boxes?" a voice said. "Three flights of stairs are quite exhausting, ya know, maybe you could bring some small things up, whilst me and Simon carry the larger boxes."

It was Darius. "Oh, sorry, Hun," Channelize replied. She had been so engrossed in her vision for redecorating the apartment, she had completely forgotten about assisting with the boxes, and there were a lot of boxes! While she had been packing them in Spain, she remembered thinking, it would be quite a task getting all of them up the fifty-four steps that led to the apartment. However, Darius had always been a hard worker and surprisingly strong for his size.

They had known each other for about four years now. They had met shortly after Channelize had moved to Spain and the chemistry between them was obvious. They spent many hours chatting over a few glasses of wine, about anything and everything. She had been quietly attracted to him from the start and she sensed he felt the same way about her.

The problem was, that he was already in a relationship and Channelize had felt it was better not to pursue him. Somehow, they had managed to remain good friends, but she knew it was best for her to move on and meet more appropriate, single candidates. Channelize, was now in her early forties, free and single, but no matter how many relationships she had with other men, she would always think about Darius. None of them had ever lived up to her expectations and were normally a disappointment in one way or the other.

"They are all a waste of space!" her mother would rage. "Why can't you meet a decent man? Someone who will look after you and respect you. If you didn't drink so much, maybe you would."

Channelize had many confrontations with her mother about the way she was leading her life but, deep down in her heart, she knew that her mother loved her and just wanted the best for her. She worried about Channelize and the frequent drinking in bars. She was constantly drawing attention to herself and causing problems when she was drunk. Her mother felt that before the 'accident' with Fabergé, her granddaughter, Channelize would never have decided to escape from reality by drinking herself into oblivion. Channelize had reached a point in her life where nothing seemed to matter any more. She had resigned herself to the fact, that she would just go through the motions with the misfits she had met. After all, she had needs, like any other women. However inadequately, they seemed to serve that purpose. Quite often, the whole sordid ordeal would leave her feeling emotionally disabled and alone, with nothing left to give.

Channelize considered her friend Amelia, to be her saviour. She had met Amelia in Angelo's, a local bar in the town. Even though Amelia had come across as quite shy and reserved in the beginning, after a while they became the best of friends, sharing everything together. They seemed to complement each other's personalities. Whilst Amelia had a, calming influence on Channelize, she helped Amelia to emerge from her protective shell and learn how to have fun.

Amelia had experienced a very traumatic year. She had suddenly found herself alone and abandoned in Spain by her husband, after a ten-year marriage.

"He just couldn't explain to me, what happened with our marriage," she said. "He just didn't want to talk to me about it. After all, if either of us were having an affair, then I think it would have been easier to understand, but we had a perfectly happy marriage. Or so I thought."

Amelia was racked with guilt for a while, constantly trying to find the answer and always believing it was something she had done. Channelize however, had been through a divorce from her son's father, several years earlier, so she tried to bring some clarity to Amelia's situation. They would spend many, what they called, 'ladies-that-lunch' afternoons together, where they would evaluate every intricate detail and always came up with the same final analysis.

"Basically, sweetie, he didn't have any balls!" they would conclude, almost in unison, and then both would burst into fits of laughter.

Over time, Amelia was beginning to find her life again. She was an attractive woman with long, black, shiny hair and large brown eyes. She had an oval-shaped face with a milky, almost baby-like skin that didn't tan easily. Amelia had never smoked and her best and most prominent features were her perfect white teeth and dazzling smile, which always lit up her face. She often wore cool, comfortable clothing in the daytime but would pull out all the stops for their Saturday girls' nights out. Her hair, nails and make-up would be perfection and her outfits would be glittery and glamorous. On one of these particular girls' nights, Amelia, met a man.

He was attracted to Amelia straight away. However, she was a little more tentative. He told her that he was from Morocco. He didn't speak much English, so they communicated in Spanish. Channelize could tell there was a definite twinkle in Amelia's eyes, which she hadn't noticed before. He introduced himself as Yusef. He was average height, good-looking with short-cropped, dark hair. He had broad shoulders, smouldering dark eyes and a tanned complexion. He was softly spoken and appeared to have gentle mannerisms. Channelize was wary of him at first, because he was Moroccan and the local residents in the town were less than respectful towards them. The Moroccans were stigmatized and tarred as being drug addicts and thieves, so unfortunately, their reputations were lower than a snake's belly!, as the saying goes. Naturally, Channelize didn't want Amelia to experience any more pain than she already had and she was still quite vulnerable. It turned out that Yusef had a good job working for a successful construction company. He told them he had been contracted with the same company for six years. Eventually, after much conversing and finding out about each other, Amelia decided to pursue his advances by exchanging phone numbers. Almost two years later, they were still crazy about each other. Amelia had even plucked up the nerve to go to Morocco to meet Yusef's family. Channelize and Amelia had many 'ladies-that-lunch days' deliberating about that. In the end, she went with him and had a great time.

During one of their many telephone conversations, Amelia had said that Yusef had never smoked cigarettes, taken drugs, or touched alcohol, due to his religious beliefs.

"What?" Channelize had exclaimed. "He's completely, teetotal! Oh dear, that's no good. That will definitely annoy the locals!" They both laughed.

Amelia had hoped that Channelize would settle down with the right person too, one day. She knew Channelize had been so hurt in the past that she had resigned herself to alcohol and misfits for the rest of her life, usually in that order. Then, a strange twist of fate occurred.

2

It was getting much harder to find employment in Spain. Some of Channelize's friends were fluent in the language yet were finding it near on impossible to find work. Even the Spanish themselves were having problems. The recession had penetrated its way through to most of the European countries and the affects had completely shattered Spain's property market. The British residents were leaving their homes in droves as they couldn't afford to pay their mortgages. The estate agencies were at their lowest ebb and struggling to sell new properties. Even the retired expats were feeling the pinch.

Channelize was sitting at the bar in Angelo's, contemplating her future. Where was she really going? she thought. What prospects did she have, continuing to live in this country? The thought of going back to England was beginning to feel like the only sensible solution. Even though she hated the weather, she knew she could find a job, and at least, make a living. The average wage in Spain was diabolical — less than the minimum wage in England. The exchange rate had affected every area of people's lives, and financially, it was getting very difficult to survive there. Channelize's thoughts turned to her mother. She was worried about leaving her. Minnie was nearly eighty years old, and not as strong as she used to be. She sat at the bar, toying with her glass of wine, with lots of thoughts and feelings racing around in her head. She was facing a dilemma that she just wasn't sure how to resolve.

Out of the corner of her eye she could see a figure approaching, "Darius!" she said, looking surprised. She turned on her bar stool to face him. "I wouldn't have expected to see you in here."

Channelize noticed that he was looking sad and depressed, which didn't seem surprising, in the present climate. Most people she knew seemed to have the same miserable expression lately. He ordered a beer and then looked directly at Channelize.

"I've broken up with Gloria," he said, sadly. "There just didn't seem to be any point staying together any more. We were always arguing and neither of us were happy."

Channelize noticed he looked a little unsure of himself. She wasn't really sure what to say, or how to feel.

"Er... are you all right... with the break up, I mean?" she asked, hesitantly.

"Yeah. Yes, I am fine with it. You and I have often talked about my feelings for her in the past, I think most people knew we wouldn't last. We haven't been happy for a while." He paused for a second and smiled, as if trying to put a brave face on it.

"I guess it just took me a bit longer to see that. Anyway, less of that. How is your life?"

Channelize tried to force a smile and raised her eyebrows. "Wow, that's a million-dollar question. I was just thinking that I need to make some changes to my life, too. Apart from the dire financial situation I'm in, I am sick of some of the ex-pats here, who have nothing better to do, than involve themselves in other people's lives. They almost enjoy other people's hardship. I mean what's that about? It's such a small town, everyone seems to know what you had for your breakfast." She replied. Darius could sense the tinge of frustration in her voice.

"And the rest!" he interrupted. They both stopped talking, looked at each other and started to laugh at the irony of the situation. It felt good. They had a few more drinks together, sharing their thoughts and feelings. Channelize knew that it had been a relief for Darius to talk. They seemed to share similar views and chatted till late into the afternoon.

Suddenly, completely out of the blue, Darius asked Channelize if she would like to join him for dinner that evening. He arranged to pick her up outside her apartment at nine o'clock. When Darius left the bar, Channelize felt strangely excited. She was actually going out on a date with Darius, or was it a date?

As she walked back to her apartment, she contemplated the situation further. Should she feel guilty? she thought, or was it much like two old friends spending some time together? It was too early for her to imagine that he still had feelings for her. Could she possibly still have feelings for him? She decided to stop reading too much into it. She felt very happy and flattered, whatever the outcome.

"Now, what should I wear?" she said to herself, as she frantically pulled half a dozen items from the wardrobe.

As Channelize enjoyed her shower that evening, she found herself mulling over the situation again in her head as she always did, jumping from one explanation to another. She thought about Lawrence, her gay friend, who she had known ever since their school days. He had often been teased and bullied because of his femininity. Channelize had too, because of her skin colour and her ethnic background. Somehow, they had become allies and remained friends through the years. She wasn't quite sure why he had jumped into her thoughts at that moment. However, Lawrence had always seemed to understand her much better than any of her female friends. He used to tell her in his camp voice,

"Darling! You spend so much time self-analysing, you forget how to just enjoy the experience."

He was right, thought Channelize. Tonight, she would just go with the flow and enjoy.

When she had finished taking her shower, she checked the clock.

"Crikey!" she screamed. "It's eight thirty, already." Channelize ran into the bedroom to quickly apply her make-up.

Darius pulled up outside the apartment at nine o'clock. He was very punctual.

Unfortunately, the same could not be said for Channelize — she was still drying her hair. She invited him inside whilst she attended to the last few strands. Perfect, she thought, as she took one last glance in the mirror. She had decided to wear her blue jeans and classic, sequined top. She wanted to be careful not to give out the wrong signals. After all Darius was still very vulnerable and possibly on the rebound. Channelize finally appeared from the bedroom. Darius was sitting down, watching the television.

"I didn't know you were a fan of the soaps?" she said, sarcastically.

"No, I'm not really," he said. 'I was just intrigued as to why you women make such a fuss about them." He smiled, his familiar cheeky smile.

"Are you ready, then?" he asked. Channelize nodded, locked the door behind her and they left. Darius was quiet in the car as they drove to the restaurant. Channelize wondered whether she should have accepted his invitation to dinner. Maybe he would have been better left alone to wallow in self-pity for a while, or maybe he was just using her in the same way as the others, just to fill in an evening? Oh god, here I go again! she thought.

The evening went well. Darius had found a very nice Indian restaurant in the centre of the town. It was uncanny how they had both ended up ordering the same item from the menu, 'curried fried shrimps'. It was apparent they both had a similar palate. They had an enjoyable evening and a few laughs. Channelize felt very comfortable being in his company again. She watched him fondly, as his face lit up whilst he talked about his life and his plans for the future. They seemed to fit like two old slippers. Channelize felt that the timing was now right, for both of them.

3

The next morning, Channelize was feeling elated over the developments with Darius the previous evening. However, she was not prepared for the shocking news that was about to be bestowed on her later that day. Channelize needed to go to the supermarket to buy some grocery supplies. It was not a chore that she relished. However, she wanted to prepare a nice meal for Darius as a gesture of thanks. As she strolled up and down the individual food aisles leisurely packing the items into her trolley, she heard her mobile phone ringing. She quickly retrieved it from her handbag. As she looked at the mobile screen, she noticed that it was Aimee, her niece, calling. Straightaway, she felt curious and rather concerned. It was unusual for Aimee to call and especially in the middle of the day. She answered.

"Hi Aimee, how are you? I haven't heard from you in a while. What's up?"

"Hi, Aunt Chanel," Aimee replied. "I'm afraid I have some bad news." She paused for a second, "Your son, Brook. He's been sent to prison. He had his court case today and was sentenced to four months."

Channelize stood in the food aisle, frozen in shock. She felt her knee's almost buckle from beneath her. She could hardly believe what Aimee had just said and desperately wanted to think that she must be playing a joke.

'Are you still there, Auntie?" asked Aimee.

"Oh, yes. Yes, of course I'm still here. You took me a little by surprise, Aimee, that's all."

Channelize gathered her thoughts and continued.

"What court case? What has he done?"

Aimee went on to tell Channelize that Brook had been found pedalling illegal drugs. Apparently, Brook had told Aimee that he had been desperate, and needed the money quickly. He had got himself involved with a notorious crowd and Aimee had advised Brook beforehand, that the mates he was hanging out with would only lead him to trouble. It seemed she had been right.

"He was really lucky, Aunt Chanel. The rest of the 'gang' received eighteen months. So, if it's any consolation, he may not have been too involved." Aimee explained.

Channelize thanked Aimee for the call and hung up the phone. There was nothing else that Channelize wanted to hear at that moment. Her heart felt like it had been ripped out of her chest. She felt really angry with Brook for his stupidity. Yet she felt a longing to be with him and tell him everything would be fine, like she used to when he was a child. Channelize stood motionless in the supermarket aisle. She tried to continue with the daily grind of shopping. However, it was impossible for her to think straight, her mind was elsewhere. She was suddenly overwhelmed by a feeling of claustrophobia. It felt as if the grocery aisles were closing in on her. She felt the eyes of the customers staring through her, judging her as if they knew. She had to get out. At that moment, Channelize needed the confines of her apartment.

As Channelize struggled home with her few bags of shopping, she couldn't stop thinking about Brook. She couldn't understand why he hadn't spoken to her about his financial problems — they had always been very close. She felt angry at herself for abandoning him and moving here to this Godforsaken town. She had allowed herself to lose touch with her only son, mentally and physically. She felt guilty and selfish for following this so-called 'Spanish dream', which hadn't turned out to be anything like she had expected. Brook was twenty-four years of age, but Channelize still considered him to be her 'baby'. She started to think about when he was a little boy and like most boys of his age, he would dream of becoming a famous football player. She remembered watching him play in the park one rainy day, with some older boys. Brook was ducking, diving and tackling them head on. She smiled to herself as she thought, then, that he looked like a little star in the making. Not that Channelize was familiar with the game but, she knew he had 'something'. He had joined a youth team when he was nine years old. His coach had always stressed to Channelize that Brook had so much potential.

"He's a natural," his coach would say proudly. He was sure that Brook would have a successful future in football. The next chapter in Brook's life was a major blow to everyone.

Suddenly all his football dreams, were shattered.

One fateful morning, Brook had jumped out of bed and run downstairs to answer the telephone. Channelize recalled the sound of him moaning and groaning at the bottom of the stairs. She had called out to him to see what was wrong, but he didn't answer. She pulled herself out of bed, thinking to herself that Brook was messing about again. Just as she reached the top of the stairs, she could see Brook lying there at the bottom. He wasn't moving, his face was pale and it looked like he had collapsed.

Channelize remembered feeling horrified. She ran downstairs as fast as she could and frantically called out to her neighbour,

"Maria, Maria! Help me, please."

Maria heard the shouting and came quickly to assist. She could tell by the look on Channelize's face that she was rigid with shock. Maria grabbed the telephone and dialled the emergency services.

"Send someone quickly!" she said, with sheer desperation in her voice. "There's a young boy here, he has had an accident! she cried. Brook was stirring and breathing heavily, he was having trouble speaking or making any sense. Channelize and Maria managed to lift Brook and lay him down onto the sofa, covering him with a blanket. It wasn't long before the ambulance arrived. After they had examined Brook, the paramedics determined that he was having some sort of seizure, but they needed to get him to the hospital straight away for more tests. Before she knew it, Brook and Channelize were whisked off to the Accident and Emergency unit, where various tests were carried out on him.

That had been fourteen years ago. Brook had been left with limited use of his right arm and leg. The doctor informed Channelize that her son had suffered a blood clot. It had been devastating news. Brook's football career had come to an abrupt end. Channelize remembered cursing God at that time. How could he just snatch away a young boy's dreams?

As time went by, Brook's mobility skills improved. He liked to be independent and prided himself on his looks and his designer clothing. He was always smiling, despite what he had been through. He learned to tie his shoes, make his own bed and feed himself, all of which he had learned through the skill of using his left hand. He still liked nothing better than to get outside with the older boys in the neighbourhood and play football. Obviously, he had lost some of his flair, but Channelize remembered thinking how remarkable and courageous Brook was, as she watched him admiringly, out of the window. There were the odd times when he would have low days, especially when he thought about the future he had lost. However, he would try to hide his pain from Channelize. But she always knew.

Channelize finally arrived at her apartment. She dropped the grocery bags down on the kitchen floor. They had felt like a dead weight. She reached for a chair and sat down slowly at the kitchen table. All the thoughts of her son had been far too much to bear. She reached for a cigarette from her handbag, but realised she didn't even have the energy or inclination to smoke it. She put the packet down on the table and placed both her hands over her face. She felt the pain erupt like a volcano from the pit of her stomach. Her tears flowed. She felt ashamed. She had failed her only son and she could only blame herself for his incarceration. If only she had been there for him.

4

Somehow, Channelize must have sobbed herself to sleep, because when she awoke, it was already late afternoon. She had slept for a good, few hours. However, as soon as her eyes were fully open, the thought of Brook in prison, seeped back into her memory. She had hoped that it was some kind of awful dream, until the reality suddenly hit her. She lifted herself up slowly from the table and started to put away the groceries. Even though she felt she had jailed Brook, it wasn't too\ late to make up for that. It was impossible to speak with him on the phone to reassure him, so she decided to write him a long letter enclosing photos of his family to support him and to let him know, that he was loved.

After all the groceries were organised, Channelize sat down to compose the letter to Brook.

First, she expressed how he shouldn't totally blame himself. Even though she didn't condone his actions, she hoped that he would learn from his mistakes. The letter was six pages long, and included family photos that she knew he would relate to. It wasn't much, she thought to herself. However, it was the best she could do for now. Channelize felt so much better writing her thoughts and feelings down on paper. There was so much she needed to say. After the letter was completed, she wondered if she should go to visit her mother and talk to her about Brook's situation but, it dawned on her that her mother would enjoy telling Channelize it was all her fault, the way Brook had turned out and what a selfish parent she was for deserting him. Channelize felt she couldn't bear to hear all of mother's derogatory comments. She didn't feel strong enough to cope with them. Also, Aimee had said that Brook preferred his grandmother not to know.

Channelize picked up the telephone, and dialled Aimee's number. She answered almost straight away.

"Hi, Aimee, it's me, Aunt Chanel. I am sorry about earlier, your news was a little unexpected." That was an understatement, thought Channelize.

"I realise that," Aimee replied, sympathetically. "I'm just sorry that I had to be the bearer of such bad news but, I had to tell you. Gran doesn't know, does she? Brook really feels ashamed of himself."

"God, no!" replied Channelize. "But it's good to know he is not proud of his actions. Aimee, I have written Brook a long letter. Do you happen to have the address of the prison?" Even saying the word prison, made Channelize feel sick to her stomach. How could her baby be condemned to such a place, she thought?

"You can send the letter to me, if you like. I can take it with me when I go to visit him on Sunday afternoon," Aimee replied.

"Thank you so much, Aimee. Do you think I should come over to England?" asked Channelize.

"Oh no, Auntie! Brook specifically said that he didn't want to see anyone from the family. Only me, of course. He will be all right Aunt Chanel. It's an open prison so he won't be locked up all the time and hopefully it won't be for long. Anyway, I will pass the letter on, I'm sure he will appreciate it," Aimee said, reassuringly.

"All right then. I will post it to you and call you again soon, Aimee. Thank you so much for being there for him, I really do appreciate that from the bottom of my heart," concluded Channelize. They said their goodbyes and hung up the phone.

Channelize felt much better having spoken with Aimee, she had always been her favourite niece.

They had both enjoyed each other's company in the past. There was only a fifteen-year age gap between them. Aimee was always bubbly and full of life. She had the type of personality to lift anyone's spirits. She was just the person that Brook needed around him, right now, thought Channelize. She decided to cancel her evening with Darius. Her stomach was too churned up over her son and she wasn't really in the right mood for cooking and socialising.

She didn't feel the need to mention anything about Brook to Darius. After all it was a family matter. She didn't want to talk about it to anyone. She was still trying to absorb all the details herself. At that moment,

Channelize rang Darius and made her excuses. They arranged a dinner date for another evening. Darius had been very understanding and hadn't pushed for any further explanation, apart from that she wasn't feeling well. However, once Channelize had heard his voice at the other end of the line, she felt the need for him to put his arms around her, embrace her tightly and tell her everything would be all right.

It was only eight o'clock in the evening, but Channelize was mentally exhausted. She decided to have an early night. She drew the curtains to block out the light and got into bed. 'Well… tomorrow's another day," she said to herself, hoping that by tomorrow, this whole mess would have disappeared. She sighed with fatigue, leaned over and switched off the bedside lamp.

5

The next morning, Channelize woke up early. She squinted, as she drew the curtains, trying to adjust her eyes to the brightness of the sunshine beaming through the windows. At least there were 'some' advantages to living in Spain, she thought to herself, as she looked out at the quirky, pineapple-trunked palm trees, growing around the terrace and the beautiful clear blue sky. The weather could always be relied upon, which was a complete contrast to England. However, Channelize did miss the seasonal climate of England. The rich, green patchwork-quilted landscape, the large, hanging willow tree's overlooking the river in the summer and the budding, cherry blossom, in the spring. It was always so excruciatingly hot in Spain — the climate was dry and humid. It was difficult for her to even achieve the basic household chores as the sweat would pour off her brow and tire her very quickly. The best place to be on days such as these, were by the pool, or relaxing on the beach. It was far too hot for walking or sports and since she was already blessed with a mixed, black and white heritage, Channelize could hardly see the point of exposing herself to the sun.

She threw on her dressing gown and slippers and

sauntered into the kitchen to have her morning ritual of English tea and nicotine and to contemplate her activities for the day. As she sipped on her tea, her eyes wandered over to Brook's letter propped up against the suitably placed candle-holder in the centre of kitchen table. She remembered it had been a gift from Vivien, one Christmas. Two thoughts flashed through her mind at that moment. Firstly, she needed to post Brooks letter to Aimee. Afterwards, she would visit Viv for a cuppa and a chat.

Vivien had been a close friend to Channelize. She was in her early fifties and was born and bred in the East End of London. She was easy-going and down to earth, there were no airs and graces with Viv. She would say it as she saw it and would never mince her words. Viv was a very independent person, she had purchased her own apartment a few years before Channelize had befriended her. At that time, the property market in Spain was booming and Viv had cornered herself a real bargain. She was a shrewd business woman with a self-reliant demeanour. She was very attractive, her hair was a honey-blonde, cut into a neat bob style. She had a healthy appetite too, and loved cooking. Luckily, she wasn't overweight, yet often complained about her midriff packing on a few pounds. She liked very simple and conservative clothes and tended to stick to earth colours to match her deep green eyes. Vivien had been a widow for years and for that reason she was susceptible to gossip and backstabbing by other female ex-pats who saw her as a threat and were jealous of her achievements. She was smart, and knew not to get involved with some of ex-pat wives, who she compared to vultures, just waiting for any old scrap or snippet of information they could get their hands on, only to use it as ammunition against her.

Vivien had led an interesting and exciting life and Channelize loved to be in her company. She never ceased to be fascinated by all of Viv's wonderful stories about the East End and the characters she had met. Her vocabulary was full of colourful language, to say the least, which Channelize had become used to over the years. However, she was fun-loving, and a really genuine person. Channelize thought that Viv was especially amusing after downing a few glasses of red wine. Her legs would wobble like jelly. One leg would head for Madrid and the other for Barcelona! There had been a couple of occasions when they would both stumble home together, linked arm-in-arm, laughing so much they could barely walk. Channelize smiled, as she thought fondly of those times.

Vivien's home was always immaculate, she was very house proud. Much effort on her part, had gone into making her home look, stylish and sophisticated. It was decorated in pastel — peach and creams. She collected small crystal glass ornaments and in one of the bedrooms she had delicately displayed all of the ornaments on her French-style, dressing table. The bed was always dressed in a cream-frilled, satin duvet, with matching pillow cases. This room was her daughters' room, when they came to stay, which unfortunately for Viv, wasn't that often. She worried a great deal about her daughters. They were both adults, in their twenties now, and her eyes would always light up when she talked about them. Vivien was so proud of them, and financially, had given them a good start in life. Like all mothers, Vivien felt inadequate and used to worry that she hadn't done the very best for her children. She hadn't had it easy herself and had raised them practically alone, after her husband died at a very young age. She had loved her husband very much and missed him terribly. Since his tragic death, she had never taken an interest in another relationship. This was just the person Channelize needed to speak to and spend time with today, she thought. They could discuss Brook's problems and she knew that Vivien would understand. She was more open-minded than her mother, and Channelize knew Viv wouldn't judge her as her mother might. Viv, often reminded Channelize of Aimee's mother, Tonie, and she enjoyed being around her.

It didn't take Channelize long to get dressed. She had prepared herself by wearing her bikini underneath her shorts. She knew that Vivien loved to sunbathe and spent her time by the swimming pool on her day off work, so no doubt, that's where she would be, thought Channelize. She kissed Brook's letter before dropping it into the post box and then headed for Viv's apartment block. As she entered the main glass entrance doors, she spotted Viv sunbathing by the pool. She approached her quietly, so as not to alarm her whilst she was sleeping.

"Viv, are you asleep?" Channelize bent down and whispered.

Viv stirred and rolled over, looking up at Channelize with a large pair of black shades covering her eyes,

"Oh, it's you, babe," she replied lethargically. "Nah, not really. I was just relaxing. Maybe I did doze off for a bit, darling, I don't fackin' remember! That's old age for ya," she chuckled. "Anyway, what you up to today? Are you going for a swim?"

Channelize turned to look at the pool. With the midday sun dancing and shimmering on the surface, the water looked a beautiful crystal blue and very inviting. Channelize nodded, 'Yeah, I think I will have a quick dip. But I wanted to talk to you about something, if you've got time?" replied Channelize, vaguely.

Vivien sat bolt upright, lowered her sun glasses to the edge of her nose and gave Channelize an inquisitive stare.

"Is it important?" she asked. "'Cause we could always go up my place and have a chat over a nice cuppa. I could make you some lunch if ya like, babe."

'Yes, please, Viv, I could murder a cuppa tea but, don't let me disturb your sunbathing. I fancy a swim first anyway," Channelize replied.

"Oh, my Lord, not at all!" Viv exclaimed, as she pulled herself up and started packing her towel, sun cream and a bottle of water into her beach bag. "I will look like a lobster if I stay out ere much longer. I've been out 'ere for two hours, and still no bloody browner." she said, whilst adjusting her swimsuit. "Guess you don't 'ave that bloody problem though, do ya babe?" she mocked, as she walked along the grass lawns and disappeared up the stairs. Vivien went up to her apartment while Channelize had a slow, relaxing swim. Luckily, the pool was empty at this time of day — all the Spaniards were at work. This was the best time to have a quiet swim because the weekends at Viv's pool were always jam-packed with families and their boisterous, noisy teenagers, showing off their amazing dive-bombing techniques, which they expected all of the visitors to appreciate? Channelize's mind and body felt relaxed after her swim, the gentle exercise had cleared her mind for a while. She sunbathed a little to dry off and then went up to see Vivien. As she made her way up the stairs to Viv's apartment, Channelize could smell the aroma of bacon and eggs sizzling from Viv's kitchen. Channelize smiled to herself as she thought how typical it was of Viv's nature to put herself out for people. Channelize opened the back door to the kitchen, "Mmm! I thought I could smell bacon," Channelize remarked, appreciatively

"Well, I was a bit peckish me self, so I thought I would whip us up a sarnie," replied Viv, flipping over the greasy bacon in the pan. "Gawd blimey! I'll never get rid of this bleedin' belly," she said, rubbing her belly like it was Alladin's Lamp, and secretly hoping it would just disappear?

"Sit ya arse down then and tell me what's up," she demanded.

6

Channelize and Viv tucked into their lunch and spoke for about two hours. She shared her thoughts and fears with Viv about Brook.

"Fackin' four months!" Viv roared. "Gawd blimey, that's a piece o' cake. He will be out in no time. He's lucky he's not doing a long stretch like some of the geezers I know. We're talking twenty, twenty-five years! In wiv some 'ard bastards too, I can tell ya!" She laughed. "Four bleedin' months!" she said again, under her breath and shaking her head in disbelief. "You've got naffin' to worry about, Chanel, that will fly by. I thought you was gonna tell me he was banged up for five or ten years!"

Channelize smiled, and felt much better.

They changed the subject and spoke about the gossip that was already going around, about Channelize and Darius.

"How did you know about our dinner date?" asked Channelize, indignantly. "Not that I wouldn't have told you, but news certainly travels fast around here, doesn't it?" Channelize looked at Viv enquiringly, waiting for her response.

They both knew the type of town this was. It was

apparent that some of the ex-pats who lived here, had too much time on their hands and nothing to do with it. They felt they had the right to sit in judgment of other people. Both Channelize and Viv had been the target of gossip over the years, most of it untrue and very hurtful.

Channelize remembered when she had first moved to the area. It had taken less than two weeks before the nasty, racist comments began to rear their ugly head. It had really upset Channelize at first. She was slurred with the label 'nigger' at least three times in one week.

It wasn't actually the name that hurt, as she knew the meaning of it. It was the fact that she hadn't been subjected to those types of derogatory comments in years, since she was a child, and that was from other children, but these were not children. These people were grown-up, mature adults! She had hoped that times had changed and she was upset that some of the English community here were still living in the Dark Ages. Their ignorance appalled her. How could people in this day and age, still think about people of colour in this way, she would often think to herself. She would try to relay her feelings to her mother, but unfortunately, due to no fault of her own, her mother didn't take it so seriously. Channelize had felt very let down by her attitude. But how could she really understand. Things like that didn't affect her. She was white. Channelize knew right from the start that she was on her own. She would have to stand up for herself, which she had done many times. However, she hadn't realised, that with hindsight, she had been a fool only to herself, and played into their hands. Her aggressive and hostile behaviour had only fuelled the fire for the gossip mongers and confirmed their thoughts about so-called, niggers. She was quickly isolated and stigmatised.

Channelize had learned very early on, to keep her friends close and her enemies closer. This was one of the reasons Viv and Channelize had become allies. They had both experienced various degrees of discrimination. In fact some of the gossip about them and other people was so far-fetched and amusing, Viv and Channelize would often split their sides laughing.

"Some of these people should write a bleedin' book," Viv would say with a giggle. "It would definitely be a, best seller. Their imaginations are so fackin' vivid!" Channelize would agree.

Channelize was intrigued. It had genuinely slipped her mind to mention the dinner date to Viv, especially since the main topic of conversation that afternoon, had been Brook.

"Well," Viv continued. "Darius's ex-girlfriend, Gloria, was in the shop the other day, and she made a point of saying that, she thought you hadn't wasted much time getting your claws into Darius, which is exactly how she put it. Someone, apparently, told her that they spotted the two of you in the Sheik Indian restaurant, having an intimate dinner together? Well, you know me, Channelize, I said to that upperty little

41

madam... 'Look! from where I'm standing, missus, you ain't with Darius any more so, what he does and with whom he does it with, really ain't none of your fackin' business?' And another thing, I said. 'Channelize 'appens to be a good friend of mine, and I know she don't need to get 'ere claws into anyone. She has loads of male admirers, so you stick that in ya pipe, and smoke it!'"

Channelize smiled, as she watched Viv's comical interpretation of the conversation, and also because of her natural loyalty and support.

"These bloody people round 'ere," Viv moaned. "Always out to start some crap about someone else. They get on me bleedin' nerves!" Her face became serious as she looked at Channelize.

'I won't be staying around 'ere much longer, meself, Chanel. I miss me little grandson and me girls so, I'm seriously thinking of getting on me bike, and going back home," she said, completely out of the blue. Viv paused for a moment and then slumped off towards the bathroom.

Channelize sat at the table, her face in shock. Viv's jovial mood had suddenly become very melancholy and she wasn't even drunk. It took Channelize a few seconds to get her head around it. Viv had often talked about going back to London when she was drunk, but she would normally forget all about it and she loved the sun. Somehow, Viv was serious this time. Channelize was aware that lately, Vivien had been getting fed up with her job in the supermarket and all the 'Chinese whispering' amongst the staff and the English community, in this small-minded town. She wouldn't tolerate a lack of respect for her private life, which she had tolerated for six years. Vivien was as close to Channelize, as any sister could be. If Viv left, Channelize knew she would be devastated.

When Vivien returned from the bathroom, her hair was styled and she had applied a little makeup. She looked at Channelize mischievously and smiled.

"Well, since it's me day off, Chanel, shall we go to Angelo's for a couple of jars?"

"Why not!" Channelize replied, enthusiastically. "Have you got a T-shirt or something I could throw on?" she asked, putting her thoughts behind her about Viv's last statement.

Angelo's, was a bar that most of the ex-pats, and locals frequented. There was a mixture of nationalities — mostly English, Norwegians, Irish and Spanish. It was quite a successful bar compared to most in the town, and Angelo normally provided some form of entertainment most nights of the week, from live Spanish music, to disco and karaoke. Angelo himself, was a lovely looking man. He was in his early forties and had a look of Rock Hudson, with distinguished grey streaks through his thick, jet-black hair. He was charismatic and good-natured. Angelo always had a way of making people feel welcome. Holiday-makers and their families would visit his bar every year, just to pay their respects. He was very good at acting like he remembered them… whether he did, or not?

They arrived at Angelo's around five o'clock. It was never really busy at that time and easy to get stools at the bar. Channelize ordered two glasses of wine. She frequented Angelo's more than Vivien so the bar staff automatically knew her.

'The usual for you, Channelize?" Roberto confirmed.

"Yes please, Roberto," she replied.

Another benefit of living in Spain, was that the wine and cigarettes were really inexpensive. That was one of the reasons, why so many people suffered with various alcohol-related problems, thought Channelize. There had been a stage when she also, could only find comfort and escapism in a drink. Now, she was beginning to learn how to overcome the abusive alcohol period in her life, it was a slow process. The times when she had been out of her head on drink, all of her deep-rooted anger would emerge. Most of the time she didn't even know what she was doing, or who she was doing it with. Alcohol had been her worst enemy. She had caused so much trouble for herself. Her mother had felt embarrassed and ashamed of her. The more inadequate and guilty she felt, the more abusive she would become. Channelize had felt, at that time, that no one cared about her, not even her mother. Eventually, through meeting good friends like Viv and Amelia, she had begun to realise that she wasn't as crazy as everyone had labelled her. Just very misunderstood.

Her real friends started to understand her, as they got to know her. They shared many of her views. They had also experience in different ways, the patronising by the ex-pats, and a similar disrespect for their lifestyles. Viv and Amelia had been her lifelines, and Channelize started to find a certain respect for herself again. She had found it difficult to rise above the criticism alone, but Viv and Amelia had taught her how. She began to realise through her friends, that it was all a game to the perpetrators. Through her temperamental outbursts, Channelize had been allowing them to win. She felt she had a solid support system now and she didn't want to let them down. Her motto was, that she would abuse alcohol when she felt like it, but she would not allow alcohol to abuse her. Channelize's biggest vice was smoking, which she had done a great deal more of in Spain. She could easily smoke twenty-five cigarettes a day compared to living in England, when a normal day would be no more than ten or fifteen at the most. Channelize was beginning to realise, like Viv, that this town and its community were destroying her, in more ways than one.

Vivien and Channelize always seemed to open up to each other when they were drinking together and after her third glass of wine, Channelize was beginning to feel happy and relaxed. They must have talked about anything and everything. They had a giggle about who was thought to be having an affair with whom, the state of the economy, Viv's grandchildren and her girls. Suddenly, out of the blue, Vivien asked Channelize the reason why she had moved to Spain. Everyone had a story with regard to how they had ended up there, but Channelize had never really discussed her story, apart from the obvious reason that her mother and stepfather had moved there. She had never wanted to divulge any other information and had always been very guarded, even with Viv. Channelize took a deep breath, she was feeling slightly light-headed from the three glasses of wine. She supported her head with her hands by carefully entwining her fingers and placing her hands underneath her chin.

"Do you really want to know?" she slurred.

"Yeah... yeah, of course I do," Viv replied, curiously.

7

Channelize steadily tried to focus her eyes on Vivien.

"I had a daughter once, Viv, I never told you that, did I?"

Viv looked surprised and shocked at the same time. "What do you mean, you had a daughter, Channel. What happened to her?" Viv asked.

Channelize continued with her story about Fabergé and how one fateful day, when she was three years old, they had decided to go and visit some friends in Nottingham. Channelize remembered how excited Faberge had been that morning.

"Mummy, are we going on a choo-choo train?" she asked two or three times over. She was so hyper, running around the living room acting like a little train. "Choo-choo!" she would whistle, swirling her little arms about.

"I'm going faster, Mummy, look, look!"

Fabergé had never been on a train before and was ready in no-time, waiting impatiently for the taxi to arrive to take them to the station. When they arrived the atmosphere was manic. Commuters rushing to and fro, whistles blowing, trains pulling in and out of the platforms. Channelize told Faberge to stay by her side, as she hadn't brought her buggy. Fabergé had insisted on being independent and was eager to walk, like a grown-up, she would say. It was only a day trip so, just this once, Channelize had allowed her to have some freedom. However, she still had the reins fastened around her chest, just in case.

They shuffled through the crowds and made their way to the ticket office. Fabergé was chattering away to herself, and Bluebell, her little furry toy monkey. She took Bluebell everywhere with her.

"Look Bluebell, a choo-choo train. You better be good or you won't go on it… will he, Mummy?" she said, as she looked up at Channelize with her beautiful, dark-brown eyes as large as saucers, surrounded by long, thick, black eyelashes, her loose curly black locks, popping out of different areas of her pink crochet hat. She had worn her best pink velvet coat today, too, with its matching bag. She had decided to keep Bluebell inside the bag. "Better keep him safe," she said to Channelize, firmly.

Channelize remembered thinking how small Faberge looked against the masses of adult people around her, but it didn't seem to faze her. She was tottering along, just like a little mini adult, and was fascinated by the noise of her little black patent shoes, clicking and tapping on the white tiles of the train station floor. She looked so cute, thought Channelize, as she watched her acting very independently.

They finally got to the ticket booth. Channelize

started sifting through her handbag to find her purse. The ticket operator was a tall, thin man, with a sharp, pointed nose and a pair of bi-focal glasses perched on the end of it. His bulbous eyes were staring over his spectacles at Channelize. He said abruptly, "Hurry up, madam. I do have a queue of people behind you… these trains don't wait forever you know." Channelize was desperately searching for her purse. She remembered using it to pay the taxi driver and hoped that she hadn't dropped it in the cab. The ticket operator started to tap his fingers on the counter, puffing and sighing.

"Come on, madam! I will have to ask you to move in a moment — people are waiting," he said, rudely. At that moment, Channelize felt like telling him where to stick his ticket, as rudeness always ticked her off but, she knew Fabergé was really looking forward to their day trip. She spotted the purse and gave the ticket attendant a triumphant glare, before looking down to reassure Fabergé that she had found it when…… Oh, my God! Where was she? Channelize's eyes widened as she looked around her. She turned to the lady behind her in the queue and said, "Excuse me, did you see that little girl with me, she was standing right here?"

The lady looked at Channelize blankly, "No," she replied. "But are you going to be long, I have a train to catch."

Channelize pushed through the queue of people, shouting Fabergé's name. A wave of panic suddenly shot through her like a bolt of lightning. She must have

49

let go of the reins for a split second, while she searched for her purse. She started to feel her heart pounding and her skin sweating. She couldn't see any sign of her. Fabergé was so small against all these people, she thought. Channelize suddenly spotted an attendant on the platform and ran over to him.

"Please, sir! Have you seen a small child wandering around here? It's my daughter. She's only three years old. She's disappeared!" Channelize screamed, frantically.

He was an old gentleman and it was difficult for him to hear her because of the noise of the trains pulling in and out of the station and the booming voice on the loud speaker making various announcements.

"What did you say, pet? the old attendant asked. Channelize repeated herself again, trying to shout as loud as she could over the noise.

Little girl?" he said, looking a bit vague. "What was she wearing?" Channelize gave him a detailed description of Fabergé, and her outfit. The attendant looked at Channelize and his face became grave and concerned. He could see the anguish on Channelize's face and immediately took her to the main office on the platform.

"Here, sit down there, miss," he said kindly, pointing to a long wooden bench. "I will put a request out over the tannoy to all members of staff, to see if they have seen her, and to check all possible places she could be. I must admit though, miss, this is not a safe place for a child that age to be wandering around alone."

The search for Fabergé continued for about three hours. To Channelize, it felt like a lifetime. She had been given a cup of tea and some reassuring words by the attendant.

"Don't worry," he said. "Kids that age have a habit of being curious, and hiding in the oddest places," he let out a little chuckle. "I have a little granddaughter of my own... she's two years old." Channelize looked up at him and tried to smile, all of her thoughts at that moment, were on finding Fabergé.

"Oh, she can be a little devil at times." He was about to continue, when a smartly dressed, statuesque women walked into the office. She was dressed in a grey skirt, and matching jacket, her black hair, styled and tied neatly in a bun. She looked official, thought Channelize, as she stood up eagerly, waiting for some confirmation of her daughter's whereabouts.

"Hello," she said, and introduced herself. "I'm Mary Vickers, the Director of Operations here," she continued. I am so sorry to hear about this terrible situation with your daughter, but I'm afraid we have covered every possible place. I have even checked with all the trains going in and out of the station in the past few hours, and she has not been seen travelling on any of them." She paused for a moment, looking at the attendant gravely. Her voice lowered as she said to Channelize, "I think we need to call in the police."

Channelize could not speak. She felt her throat

tighten as if she was physically being strangled by Mary Vickers' words. Any strength she had at that moment, drained from her body. Her knees buckled, forcing her to sink back down onto the bench. The tears flooded out.

"Please! Please! help me," she cried. "I need my little girl... I need Fabergé!" While Mary Vickers sat down to comfort Channelize, she signalled to the attendant to call the police.

As Channelize told her story, Vivien was completely captivated. She had never even suspected that Channelize had another child. She had never mentioned her before, even when Viv had talked constantly about her own grandchildren. Her heart went out to her. Channelize took a deep breath as her eyes glazed with tears. She was about to continue when Vivien interrupted.

"Listen, babe, you don't have to talk about this if you don't wanna."

Channelize nodded and said, "Actually, Viv, it's good to talk. 'It happened, and I have to face it now."

"So... what happened next?" Viv said, cautiously, "Did someone take her?"

"No... maybe I could have dealt with that... in time. At least there would have been a slim chance of seeing her again." Channelize paused, and took a deep breath.

"It was an accident, and Fabergé was killed." Viv gasped with horror.

"They found her little pink bag in the tunnel and a few yards along the track they found…" her voice choked, by now she was trembling with the pain of reliving the ordeal.

"Bluebell… They found Bluebell," she repeated, hiding her face with the palms of her hands.

"Apparently, the police assumed that Bluebell must have blown along the track, and Fabergé had gone after him. Unfortunately, she had gone onto the track and into the tunnel. She was so small and it was so dark, no one would have seen her."

Channelize's voice trailed off as she stared into her wine glass. She was reliving the nightmare of that day all over again. Inside, the feelings came flooding back into her mind. She broke down, the tears streaming down her cheeks.

"It was all my fault! If only I had taken her buggy or watched her more closely while I found that stupid, bloody purse."

Viv found herself drawn to Channelize at that moment. She gently reached out and placed her hand onto Channelize's shoulder, trying to comfort her. She told her not to live with the blame, and spoke of how all her life she had done the same thing, after her husband had died so suddenly.

"It's so easy to do that," she told her, but it will never bring them back.

Channelize tried to compose herself, "I know, Viv," she said sniffling. But I loved her so much."

Channelize had given birth to Fabergé at thirty-six years of age. She wasn't expecting to have another child after Brook, but she was so happy to have a daughter. She had always wanted a girl and Faberge was a beautiful child. She had met Faberge's father in a nightclub. His name was Paul. He was tall, dark, handsome and charming. She wasn't sure about him at first, because she had heard so many unhealthy rumours about his past and the shady people he was involved with. However, he had always been honest with her. After a while, she felt she wanted and needed to trust him. She fell pregnant very quickly and things between them were great, in the beginning. He was excited about the baby and wanted to help in any way he could. Channelize knew that Paul smoked 'grass' occasionally. However, she was not aware of the extent, or of his cocaine addiction. He always seemed to act pretty normal around her. Obviously, over time, the cracks started to appear within their relationship. Paul's behaviour had started to become neurotic. He would cause arguments over the slightest and simplest things. He would fly into uncontrollable rages and become violent and destructive, smashing windows, furniture and anyone who got in his way. It was frightening for Channelize. She was forced to call the police on a number of occasions to protect herself and her children until it came to the point when, the social service department of the police force, gave her a warning. If the situation continued, and the children were deliberately forced to endure these violent conditions, they would have no other alternative than to remove the children from the household. One of the female officers put it to Channelize, "The atmosphere in this household, is similar to standing your children on the edge of a cliff, knowing they could fall off at any moment. That would be a dangerous thing for any mother to do. Do you see Channelize? That is exactly what you are doing to your children. Could you ever do that… if you were a loving, caring mother?"

"No! Never" Channelize protested.

"Then get them out of here, my sweet, for their safety and for yours!" she insisted.

This was the wake-up call that Channelize needed. It was imperative! She needed to get away from Paul as soon as physically possible. He had become totally unbearable to live with. Every day she feared for her life, and more so for Brook and Fabergé. They were her life, and there wasn't a man in the world who could compete with the love she had for the two of them. One night, an opportunity had presented itself to Channelize. Paul was out of his head and high on drugs. He had knocked himself out and was slumped across the bed, fast asleep. Thinking of what the police women had said, Channelize decided to seize the opportunity, and escape from Paul, once and for all.

She hurriedly packed a few clothes for the children. Then, she telephoned her sister, Tonie, who lived in a village a few miles away. She briefly explained her situation, and pleaded with Tonie to let her stay for a while with the children. Tonie agreed and offered to help in any way she could. Channelize woke Brook, and wrapped Fabergé in a warm blanket. She stirred only a little and then fell straight back to sleep, hugging her favourite toy monkey. Channelize secured the children into the car. Her heart was pounding, as she feared Paul would wake up at any moment. She continuously checked the light in his bedroom window, while she quickly secured the children's safety straps, hoping and praying that Paul would not wake up. She closed the door quietly on the driver's side, switched on the engine and sped off, into the night. She drove like the wind, and never looked back.

Tonie, held an influential position within the Social Services department. She managed to provide them with a safe house, near to where she lived. Channelize never heard from Paul again.

After experiencing such an ordeal, Channelize swore to herself that she would always protect her children and never put them in any type of danger again. All three of them had been so much happier and more relaxed in their new life. Channelize found herself feeling very protective of Fabergé, especially after Brook's accident. However, on the fateful day of her death, she wasn't there to protect her, and she could never forgive herself.

Channelize continued pouring her heart out to Viv.

"Anyway, after it was all over — you know, the

inquest and all of that — I needed to get away. I was having a very hard time. I was on all kinds of pills, sedatives, anti-depressants, you name it. To be honest, Viv, none of it helps, does it?".

Viv nodded in agreement. She had also been there, done it and brought the T-shirt, so to speak. Channelize continued.

"So, my mother asked me to come out to Spain. She thought it would be good for me for a while — a change of scenery and a new start. She was really supportive at that time, Viv, and really tried to help me get through it but, unfortunately, coming to live here was not the answer. I had too much anger inside me and self-hate. I just turned to the bottle. I guess it helped to numb the pain for a while, a place to escape to. A place where I didn't have to be responsible for my actions. But that's when all the gossip started. People began to judge me, when they didn't know and understand me, or my life."

Viv listened and nodded sympathetically. She felt she was the only person who could relate to Channelize.

Viv knew Channelize had entertained more than her fair share of unscrupulous male admirers. She was a prime target for the low-lifes, users and abusers, because she was single and attractive with a healthy, athletic figure. She had large, brown, sad eyes, and full lips. Her hair was jet black, long, thick and curly. Her father was of Cuban origin and when Channelize slicked her hair back, tight to her head, she would look very Latin American, in Viv's eyes. Channelize had spoken to Viv on several occasions about her relationships with the opposite sex. Sometimes, their conversations had kept Viv highly amused. There was always some kind of excitement, or drama going on in Chanel's life, which made her interesting, funny and totally carefree. Her biggest problem was alcohol. Channelize had been drinking excessively, and it was only now, that Viv knew why.

There had been another relevant guy in Channelize's life, back then. Viv had known him quite well as he lived in the same apartment block as she did. His name was Yanni. Viv remembered thinking, he was very much in the 'same place' as Channelize was at the time.

He, too, had a chip on his shoulder about certain aspects of his life — he was very hard to get close to. Yanni was the athletic type and Viv had often seen him in the pool, and been fascinated by his dolphin-flips and dives. He usually made an extra effort when he was aware that she was admiring his technique. He was good-looking, fit and tanned all over.

Viv would often say to Channelize, as they admired him from the balcony, "Gawd blimey! If I was only a few years younger? Unfortunately babe, it's not me he's after — it's you, he's got his eye on!"
Channelize would blush, and brush it off. However, one hot, sunny day, as Channelize and Viv was sitting outside on the patio drinking coffee, Yanni came outside and shouted across to Viv, "Hola, como estas? »

"Muy bien, Yanni. Y tu?" she replied,

"Com si com sa. All right, I guess," he said.

As he spoke to Viv, his eyes wondered over to Channelize, anticipating some kind of response from her.

"Say saminck then!" encouraged Viv, kicking Channelize underneath the table. Channelize looked over.

"Oh... er, hola," she said sheepishly.

Well, that was the start of it all. Viv remembered thinking, there's a flicker of chemistry here, as she watched it grow into a hot burning flame.

8

A relationship developed between Yanni and Channelize, soon afterwards. They had so much in common and spent every waking minute together. Viv observed a change in both of them. He appeared to be less arrogant and more approachable, whilst Channelize appeared relaxed and comfortable in his presence. They often visited Viv's apartment, and Viv was always amused by the cocktail of funny stories Yanni would tell about his family and his homeland in Northern Spain. Vivien noticed Yanni was like a different person now. He was lively, funny, warm and respectful. It was obvious to Viv that he made Channelize very happy. In Viv's opinion, he was the first, genuine man that Channelize had met in a long time.

He was an excellent cook, too, and enjoyed showing off his culinary skills, preparing intimate, candlelit dinners for the two of them. Afterwards, he would serenade Channelize with different styles of music, played on his guitar. Music was one of Yanni's passions and occasionally he would perform in the local bars to earn a living. He led a fairly simple and frugal existence. However, he was more than happy to share anything he had with Channelize.

Channelize was an easy person to talk to. She would listen endearingly, whilst Yanni opened up to her about his life in prison, his estranged relationship with his father and the love he had for his ex-girlfriend who died of cancer, a few years ago. Tormented by this mixed bag of emotions, it had turned him into a very lonely, angry and bitter person. Yanni felt it was safer for him to detach himself mentally and physically from human emotion. He was self-sufficient and independent. He felt he didn't need anyone — hence his nickname 'The Cat'. His closest friends and confidants were his mother and brother. He had made a pact with himself not to let anyone get inside his head, as he would say.

The summer months passed by and their relationship flourished. Christmas was just around the corner and Channelize had decided to invite a few friends over to her apartment for Christmas dinner.

"Well, I hope I'm the guest of honour," Viv had said, cheekily,

"Of course you are, your Highness!" exclaimed Channelize amusingly, holding the corners of her skirt to curtsy.

It was early Christmas morning. Yanni had stayed over on Christmas Eve, to help prepare the Christmas lunch. It was exciting for him because he wasn't accustomed to the traditional, English way of celebrating Christmas. Everything was prepared. The duck was basted and sizzling away nicely in the oven with the turkey and roast potatoes. There were four guests expected, Suzanne and her partner Steve, Vivien and Amelia. Yusef was unable to come as he had gone to visit his family in Morocco. Suzanne had said she would provide the dessert and Viv and Amelia were bringing the wine. Yanni had prepared a selection of traditional Spanish foods, as a treat. The Christmas lunch was a big success. Yanni entertained the guests by playing a few seasonal songs on his guitar, which they had enjoyed. Everyone had drunk their fair share of wine, including Channelize. All the guests were feeling quite boisterous and merry by seven o'clock in the evening. Amelia suggested playing a game of Twister. However, they were so uncoordinated, especially Viv, and far too busy splitting their sides with laughter at Steve's antics and quirky positions on the mat, they decided to give up. Right on cue, Viv made a suggestion.

"Let's go to Angelo's, to finish off a really superb day," she slurred, waved her arms in the air and then dismissed herself by falling in a heap on the floor.

A few days went by after the Christmas celebrations. Channelize was concerned as she hadn't heard or seen anything of Yanni. She wondered if he had been offended by the antics and behaviour of her friends on Christmas day. After all, he was from a completely different culture, she mused.

However, she wasn't going to apologize for it and she certainly wouldn't be chasing him. She decided she would just bide her time and wait to see what happened. That evening, she walked down to the Ice Bar, which was just on the corner of her street. It was a quiet, intimate little bar, which was perfect as Channelize felt like being alone with her thoughts. She ordered a glass of white wine and was just about to take a sip from the glass when she saw Yanni walking past the window. He looked directly at her, lowered his eyes and carried on walking. Channelize was bemused, upset and very annoyed. What the hell was he playing at? she thought.

She knew he must have seen her as the bar was very well lit and almost empty, apart from a couple, chatting and drinking at the bar. Besides, she had distinctly felt their eyes connect. He was acting very strange. He had deliberately ignored her and she was livid.

Channelize had always known that Yanni was prone to mood swings, she had often sensed a dark side to his personality. Now, she was even more curious as to whether he was hiding something.

9

It had been nearly a week and Channelize still hadn't heard a word from Yanni. She decided to share her thoughts with Vivien.

"I don't understand him, Viv. He seems to blow hot and cold. If he doesn't want to continue having a relationship with me why not just tell me and put me out of my misery, or is this some type of game he plays?" Channelize asked, desperately.

She had been experiencing sleepless nights and worrying herself sick. Her emotions were all over the place.

"I told you he was a bit of a dark horse, Chanel. He plays his cards very close to his chest, that one. That's probably why he don't 'ave no girlfriend, replied Viv. "I admit he did seem to be different with you. Almost human!" Viv pondered. "I don't know what's eating him, babe?"

Channelize slumped down onto Viv's sofa and sighed. The whole situation was becoming mentally exhausting.

"Neither do I, but I need to find out. Having this on my mind will spoil my New Year's Eve! I think I will go over there," she added.

Channelize jumped up and peered out of Viv's window where she had a good view of Yanni's apartment.

"He's home now. The lights are on. I think I'll go over there and try to get to the bottom of this," said Channelize, wilfully. Viv wished her luck.

"Let me know what 'appens, won't you babe? I'm 'ere if you need me," shouted Viv, behind Channelize, as she took off like a bat out of hell. Channelize turned briefly and nodded.

"Don't worry, Viv, this shouldn't take long."

Channelize felt slightly apprehensive as she knocked on Yanni's door. She was determined to find out what his problem was, for her own peace of mind. She was no stranger to disappointment, she thought. If it was the worst scenario, she would have to chalk yet another one down to experience. Her heart was thumping. She was praying that Yanni was different.

She took a deep breath and knocked on the door. It took a few minutes before he opened it. It seemed she had just woken him.

"Ola, sorry, did I wake you?" she asked.

"No… no. I was just lying down trying to think about things," he replied guiltily, trying to avoid her gaze. He held the door open wider and beckoned Channelize to come in. She was curious. What things exactly, had he been thinking about? It sounded ominous and she was almost afraid to ask, but, somehow, the words just fell out of her mouth.

"Was it anything to do with us and the reasons why you have been avoiding me?" she asked abruptly, standing defensively, with her arms folded.

He looked at her face with shame in his eyes, almost as if he knew he had not been fair to have treated her so badly. He slowly extended his arms to her. His deep, smouldering brown eyes always managed to mesmerise her. She walked rigidly toward him, his eyes were willing her and pulling her towards him, as if she were attached to an imaginary length of string. He held her in his arms tightly. She had missed him. His masculine smell melted her body with his closeness. However, she still felt anger towards him for playing with her emotions and angry with herself, for trusting. If only he knew how she had tormented herself for the past few days.

"I'm afraid, I have fallen in love with you, Channelize," he said, quietly.

She looked into his eyes, not really knowing how to respond. Her emotions were mixed up. Every time she had opened up her feelings to someone, it had never worked out and her heart was left in tatters. Yanni was different in every way. She didn't feel he would say something like this, if he wasn't serious. He continued to hold her, stroking her face tenderly. "That's the reason I have been avoiding, or rather, hiding from you. I needed space. I was confused and even angry at myself for allowing this to happen, but I can't keep running. I could hide from you, Channelize, but my feelings would not allow me to hide from them. They just kept resurfacing, over and over in my head."

"I understand," Channelize replied,

"I feel a great deal for you too, Yanni, but I'm not sure if it's love," she replied, sympathetically. "I have to be honest with you, I'm not even sure whether I am capable of love any more, or even if I know what it is?"

"Don't worry about that," he said, slowly placing one finger on her lips, suggesting he didn't want to hear any more. "I just had to tell you how I feel. It's been a long time since I felt like this about anyone. I'm glad that I can still have those feelings and I'm glad that I have these feelings for you."

He kissed her gently and passionately as they lay on the sofa, entwined in each other's arms. Channelize always felt safe and warm with Yanni but, for the first time since she'd known him, she could sense his vulnerability. They never spoke another word to each other for the rest of the evening. He held her close to his chest, she could feel his heart beating like a little drum. It was soothing. They quietly fell asleep in each other's arms.

Over the next few months, Yanni and Channelize were almost inseparable. They went shopping together, cooked together, played around in the pool together. He was loyal and protective over her. Like all couples, they would have their arguments. Vivien would watch them verbally tear each other apart, but she knew they were both passionate and headstrong people. Usually, it wasn't long before they patched things up and fell in love, all over again. Yanni couldn't stay away from Channelize for long.

Channelize also became closer to her mother, who liked the fact that she had settled down with someone who could, as she would say, 'tame' her daughter. Minnie liked Yanni, too, he would often, do little jobs around her apartment, and as poor as he was, he would never take any money from Minnie for his labour. They both had the utmost respect for each other.

Yanni had found a job in the Construction Business, which boosted his finances and his confidence. They hadn't been going out much due to their finances and would normally just share a cheap bottle of wine whilst Yanni serenaded Channelize on his guitar, but tonight they were going to a new club in the town. Channelize was so excited as she told Viv how much she was looking forward to a night out.

"Apparently, Viv, there will be a few amateur live bands playing, and Yanni is hoping to get a regular evening slot for himself," Channelize said, gushing with excitement.

They arrived at the new club around eight-thirty. The place was buzzing with people and various hopefuls were waiting to perform. They had named the club The Waterfall. It was decorated with large fan-backed wicker chairs, sporting jungle-print cushions. The lighting was subdued and romantic. Small tealight candles were delicately placed on each table.

The Waterfall had a relaxing, warm feel about it. In the main entrance, along one wall, was a simulated water fall, it was beautifully lit, and very realistic. The background was a painting of a rainforest with tropical trees, large colourful parrots and various tropical birds perching. Small hidden tubes along the top of the painting caused the water to cascade down the wall and into a pebbled brook. It was a spectacular feature. The Waterfall had charisma and wasn't too overstated. Both Yanni and Channelize were very impressed. The majority of the clientele were Spanish, which made a change for Channelize. She liked to mix with the local Spanish people. The evening started to swing into action and Yanni got the opportunity to perform on his guitar. He was elated to perform in front of a live audience, and people who appreciated his music style. They spent a few hours at the club, watching the other artists. It was getting late, so they both agreed to drop in to Angelo's on the way home, for one last drink.

When they arrived at Angelo's bar, they were both feeling euphoric. It had been good for both of them to experience something different. Yanni had been feeling independent and as proud as a peacock to be able to treat Channelize to a good quality wine, instead of the normal cheap plonk they could normally afford. They had both been quite indulgent.

Whilst Yanni was ordering their last drinks and chatting at the bar with Roberto about the new club. Channelize was suddenly approached by one of her 'misfits' from the past. She tried to avoid his eyes, but unfortunately., he caught sight of her. It was soon obvious to Channelize that he was highly intoxicated as she watched him stumble towards her and clumsily place his arm around her shoulder.

"'Ello, darling. Long-time no see, give her a drink!" he shouted rudely, and beckoned to Roberto. Roberto looked at the man with contempt and chose to deliberately ignore him. "Oi, Garçon! Over here, and give this lady a drink on me!" he shouted again, at the same time, rubbing his hand suggestively along Channelize's spine. She felt uncomfortable and tried to take his arm from around her neck but, he was a large, heavy man and totally uncoordinated. She noticed that Yanni had observed the two of them. He looked angry. His eyes pierced and locked onto the drunken man like a preying panther. Channelize knew that she had to do something before things got out of control. She finally managed to release the man's heavy arm from around her shoulder, and said casually, "Look, I'm with someone. I don't want a drink. Thanks all the same." Her politeness was lost on him. He was obnoxious and insistent and showed no sign of respect for Yanni or for Channelize. It was too late! Yanni had grabbed the man by the collar of his shirt, pulling him swiftly away from the bar and Channelize. He continued to drag him through the bar and outside into the street. It all happened so quickly. Roberto, the bar manager looked confused by the commotion, and turned to Channelize.

"What's going on?" he said curiously. Channelize looked embarrassed.

"I don't know, but I had better go and find out," she replied.

"Call me, if Yanni needs a hand with that putta!" he shouted, as Channelize ran out of the door.

Across the street in nearby waste ground, Channelize could see two figures in the darkness. She could tell by his silhouette that Yanni was one of them. They were fighting and throwing punches at each other. Yanni was ducking and diving, as the man was punching into the air. She ran over, calling out to Yanni, "Stop, stop this, please!"

Yanni quickly glanced at her and shouted fiercely, "Go inside!"

As he did so, the man picked up a large rock from the waste ground and aimed to plunge it into Yanni's head.

"Look out!" Channelize shrieked.

Just at that moment, Yanni ducked. He kicked the man to the ground and started punching him, relentlessly. Channelize turned away in disgust. She couldn't watch this any more, it was all so violent. It appeared Yanni had the upper hand. She walked back into the bar and looked at Roberto,

"Give me a drink, please, Roberto," she said.

She sat at the bar and waited. After five minutes had passed, Yanni walked in and sat beside her. She noticed his hand was cut and there were blood stains splashed all over his shirt. She looked at him, waiting for some kind of explanation. Very coolly, he ordered a drink from Roberto. They spoke a few words to each other in Spanish, which Channelize didn't understand, then he turned to look at her. She was aware of his eyes, those dark, smouldering eyes had become strange and threatening. He looked vicious. After a short pause, he spoke in a very slow manner and said, "Now... he knows I am dangerous and you will, too, if you ever speak to him again!"

For the first time, Channelize had seen a side to Yanni that she had never seen before. She knew this was a warning. Would she be the next one to suffer a beating like that? Was he that insecure and jealous that he would never allow her to speak to any of her 'genuine' male friends again? She stared at him, without speaking, her body rigid. She felt unnerved. The old alarm bells of the past were ringing in her head as she started to re-evaluate Yanni. She had seen his temper and it had made her feel very uneasy. He acted arrogantly and wouldn't even discuss the matter with her, or what had happened to the drunken man. All sorts of things went through Channelize's mind at that moment. Had he killed him? Oh my God! she thought. What if he was lying in a pool of blood somewhere on the verge of death? At that split second, Yanni reminded her of Paul, Fabergé's father. Possessive and controlling. She had always felt protected with Yanni but now, maybe he was the person she should fear the most?

10

After the previous evenings dramas with Yanni, Channelize had decided to spend some quality time with her mother. She hadn't seen her since the New Year's Eve party at Angelo's, which had been a great success. It had been good to see Minnie and her stepfather, Herbert, enjoy themselves. There had been party hats, streamers and all the trimmings laid on for a great New Year's Eve celebration. Angelo's had been crowded. It had always been a ritual in Spain, to try to eat all twelve grapes, before the clock struck midnight. Apparently, it was a very old tradition and was meant to bring the person good luck for the following year. Yanni hadn't joined them for the celebrations as he had been feeling under the weather and suffering with various influenza symptoms, so Channelize had gone out with her mother, Herbert and her friend Amelia. They had enjoyed themselves immensely. However, a week had passed and Channelize had been feeling quite guilty. Also, she had other thoughts on her mind about Yanni that she was hoping to discuss with her mother. It was the weekly market today so, before Channelize went to see her mother she had decided to buy her a bunch of flowers as a peace offering.

As she walked toward the market, Channelize spotted Herbert, her stepfather. He was struggling to hold several shopping bags in his hands and leaning on a large, white van that was parked in the street. As Channelize got closer to Herbert, she began to feel more concerned. His face appeared drained of all its colour. His skin, which was normally a shiny, chocolate-colour, looked pale and grey. He was unsteady on his feet and seemed to be breathing heavier than normal. Channelize ran up to him and tried to support him. He was a large man, heavy-set and in his late sixties.

"What's wrong, Herbert? Don't you feel well?" Channelize inquired. Herbert didn't respond. He wasn't able to speak at that moment. He just looked at her, almost like a frightened child, or a scared puppy. Channelize had never seen Herbert look scared before. He had always been a confident, almost arrogant, person. She knew he was in desperate trouble. She looked around anxiously for someone to assist her, but the market was very busy. All the people were preoccupied with their shopping. There wasn't anyone she knew, in sight. How could she get him home? she thought. He was too big to carry and she didn't want to leave him there, while she went for help, fearing that he may collapse. He was barely holding himself up as it was. Channelize was very frightened and tried to collect her thoughts. He was only one street away from his apartment block, she would try to see if he could walk slowly, with her assistance. At least he would be home, and Minnie could call a doctor.

"Herbert," she said calmly, "If I take your bags, could you manage to walk with me?"

He nodded his head, still struggling for the breath to actually speak. Slowly, Channelize started to ease him into an upright position. She took the heavy weight of the shopping bags, as Herbert started to slowly and carefully, put one foot in front of the other. He was a very proud man. Channelize knew that he would be feeling very embarrassed by the fuss he would feel he had caused. They cautiously manoeuvred along the pathway and down the street. As they approached the corner where the apartment was, Herbert stopped, took a deep breath and said,

"I'm all right now, you can go. I can manage from here."

Channelize immediately insisted that she continue with him until he was safely inside the apartment, but he wasn't having any of it. His stubborn nature started to emerge. He had made his decision and it didn't matter how much Channelize protested, she knew he wasn't going to change his mind. He was beginning to get himself stressed out and agitated by her 'fussing over him', as he put it. Channelize reluctantly dropped the shopping at the gate, she turned to him and said, "Are you sure, Herbert. I just want to help. You're not well."

Herbert nodded his head profusely, "No, no!" he said, adamantly.

With that, he picked up the bags and slowly

manoeuvred towards the main entrance door.

As she watched him shuffling along, Channelize was, for a split second, very annoyed with him. "Silly, stubborn, old fool!" she said to herself, under her breath.

Then, watching him go through the door and slowly walk down the small corridor, a sudden, very grave feeling came over. He looked so weak and pathetic. She felt her eyes well up with tears. "Poor old thing," she said to herself, again. "God help him, what would any of us do without him, especially Mother? Oh yes, mother! Channelize suddenly remembered.

She contemplated whether or not to tell her mother about the dire situation with Herbert. Obviously, he didn't want to worry her unnecessarily, so maybe she should just wait and see how he was later?

Channelize pottered around the market for a while. All the stalls were beginning to pack up their wares. She didn't have much money anyway, and her thoughts were still concerned with Herbert. She decided to just buy a small bouquet of white carnations. She knew Minnie liked them. She started to make her way back to her mother's apartment. As she approached the top of the street, her eyes widened. She could see a red- and-white-coloured ambulance, which appeared to be parked outside her mother's apartment block.

"Oh my God!" she said to herself, as she picked up her pace and ran faster down the street towards the waiting ambulance, her heart pounding. As she got closer, she could see Herbert being carried out on a stretcher, with her mother following close behind.

"What's happened, Mum?" she cried out as she approached the gate.

Minnie looked at Channelize, her face filled with worry and shock. "They think he's had a stroke," she replied. "I have to go to the hospital with him."

The paramedics were ushering Minnie to get into the waiting ambulance. "Rapido, rapido!" one shouted.

Minnie, quickly got into the ambulance and they closed the door.

Channelize was left standing on the street, alone. The ambulance turned on its siren and sped off into the distance. It had all happened so fast, she wasn't quite sure how or what, to feel. It was a similar feeling to when it had happened to Brook. She questioned herself as to why she had left Herbert earlier. She should have been more insistent. She felt sorrow for her mother and wondered how this trauma would affect her life. It was sure to take its toll on her, at her age. Channelize felt useless.

"So much for old Spanish traditions, and lucky grapes," she said to herself, subconsciously looking down, and talking to the carnations. She felt deflated, and leant onto Minnie's gate, there was nothing she could do, but wait.

Herbert stayed in the hospital for two weeks. The type of stroke he had suffered, was much worse than anyone had anticipated. The doctor had told Channelize and her mother that Herbert had been affected on either side of his brain, which was rare and unusual. He had been very lucky to be alive. Herbert was unable to walk or speak and would need constant assistance with eating, drinking, changing... the list was endless. It was almost unbearable to listen to the prognosis. Channelize looked at her mother with concern. They both realised at that moment, that it was going to take much patience, hard work, and tender, loving care, to get through the times ahead. Herbert would never be the same again. There were many tears, fears and doubts. However, Channelize was amazed by her mother's attitude. She was Irish and Channelize had always known that her mother was as tough as an old boot! And true to form, over the next few difficult months, Minnie really proved to Channelize just how tough and courageous she really was.

11

Six months had passed since Herbert had suffered his stroke. Most of Minnie's friends had been surprised that Herbert had pulled through at all. Channelize knew it was only the love and the unbreakable bond between them, that had kept Herbert going for so long and also, the sheer, bull-headed attitude that Minnie had adopted, that had kept her going, too. Minnie was positive that Herbert would walk again and none of the specialists would, or could, tell her any different.

Channelize would often observe Minnie and Herbert together and feel in awe of them, which was a very odd emotion, due to their circumstances. She would listen to her mother talking to Herbert with her bossy, no-nonsense tone of voice, saying, "All right, Herbert. Time to get this meal down you, and then we will get you to the hairdressers tomorrow, to get that mop of hair, cut. Look atcha, your beard's as long as Farder Christmas'!"

Herbert would look up at her, with his sad, docile eyes, and smile in his own way. Channelize thought it strange, that on his return from hospital six months ago, the only word he could say was, 'Minnie'. Since then, he'd added to his vocabulary slightly and it was possible to have a short conversation with him. Unfortunately, the effects of the stroke were still very visible. He was still unable to control the expulsion of saliva that would dribble from the corner of his mouth. Minnie would joke about that, too, she'd say, "Now look atcha! Do I have to put a bib on ya?" as she gently wiped him clean.

Channelize really admired her mother's strength and commitment. There was so much work that Minnie had to do, now that Herbert was so sick. Every morning she would prepare and administer Herbert's daily injections and every morning and evening she would bathe him, feed him, lift him into his wheelchair and push him into the bedroom, tucking him lovingly into bed, as if he were a small child. People stopped, asking how he was, after a while. They eventually lost interest and moved onto other issues about other people's misfortunes. They very rarely asked Minnie, how she was coping. Each day, the same routine would start all over again, it was a twenty-four-hour job, but Minnie was so independent, she would never dream of asking anyone for help.

Channelize would help with the other household chores, like cleaning, washing and even making the odd meal. It was so tiring for Minnie to keep up with the chores and take care of Herbert, too. Channelize had noticed that Minnie was rapidly losing weight. She was tiny in height compared to Herbert, but in the past, she had always had a good appetite for food and had plenty of meat on her bones. Her hair was thick and bleached blonde, which had been highlighted by the sun. She had a full, round face and a natural, creamy-coloured Irish complexion, which was almost wrinkle-free and flawless. But now the stress of the whole ordeal was beginning to show. Channelize would have to force her mother to eat, as she appeared gaunt and fragile. Minnie had enjoyed dancing and was enrolled in a weekly dance class. She also liked walking and would often take a stroll along the beach and breathe in the healthy sea air. However, now Minnie's whole life revolved around Herbert. She hardly had a life of her own any more. Channelize would make sure Minnie pampered herself at least once a week, and would always arrange her weekly appointment at the hair salon.

Channelize was visiting Minnie one afternoon and forced her mother to sit down on the balcony for a cup of tea and a chat.

"We haven't had a chat for a while now, ma'm. You're always so busy with Herbert. How are you feeling?" Channelize asked.

Minnie sighed, and rubbed her eyes. 'Well... I'm coping. We will both get through it, I pray to God, anyway," she replied lethargically.

Channelize noticed that underneath Minnie's eyes were dark circles and puffiness. No doubt through lack of sleep, thought Channelize. Quite often in the middle of the night Minnie would have to get up out of bed, to take Herbert to the toilet. Channelize was really worried about her mother's health.

"But, how do you do it, ma'm?" Channelize continued, "At your age, surely it's too much. Maybe, you should think about going to England, you would get a lot more support and assistance for you and Herbert," Channelize said, appealing to her mother to think about it.

"Herbert loves the sun out here and it's good for him. It reminds him of his homeland in the West Indies," she remarked. "What, in God's name, would he have in England? He would probably freeze to death in that rotten dismal and cold climate."

She rubbed her apron with her hands and started to clear away the cups. Channelize watched her busying about, and got the impression that Minnie was already feeling guilty because she had taken five minutes respite.

"Oh, no! When we were married and took those vows, we said, 'for better or for worst', and so be it," she said, with conviction.

That was how Minnie was, and Channelize knew there was no changing her. Deep down, she felt that Minnie and Herbert would be so much better off, physically and financially, if they left Spain, and the sooner the better. Channelize, was beginning to believe that this town was jinxed. Nearly everyone she knew had experienced some type of tragedy, one way or the other, and the situation was only getting worse.

Her mother and Herbert had retired to Spain five years ago, with the vision of a 'dream life'. They purchased a beautiful home together, enjoying the sun and the golden beaches. Herbert used to say to Channelize, that living in Spain was like... 'Christmas, every day!'. He was so happy there. He had his local bars where he had made friends and everyone knew him. He was a gentle giant and very generous. Nothing would please him more than taking Channelize and other members of the family to eat in the finest restaurants. The weather suited him too, the warm climate reminded him of the Caribbean.

During those times, it appeared Minnie and Herbert had it all. They had an ample amount of money to spend, a good social life and were happy in their retirement, until this unfortunate and unexpected illness, had completely turned their lives around. How could life be so cruel? Channelize often thought, as she watched her mother struggling to 'wait' on Herbert's every need. Then, she would observe those little gestures of love between them and think to herself, finally, now I understand what 'real love' is. She'd witnessed it every day, between Minnie and Herbert. A loyalty, commitment, strength and faith in each other, which never faltered, even under these very extreme and adverse circumstances. Channelize couldn't help but admire them both. She realised the words... 'For better or for worse', were truly demonstrated between the two of them.

Channelize felt saddened, as she assumed that with Yanni, or maybe any other man in her lifetime, she may never experience a love as remotely unique, or as special as theirs.

Shortly after Herbert's stroke, Channelize had discussed with Yanni that she would need to spend more time with her mother. She realized Minnie would need her support more than ever. Admittedly, Yanni had been understanding and sympathetic towards Minnie's plight and offered to help in any way he could. He did love Channelize in his own way, and somehow, she never questioned that. However, she was afraid of him and his impulsive behaviour. When he was in good spirits, he could be the sweetest person anyone could ever meet, but he was a, Jekyll and Hyde character. His 'dark side' was prone to paranoia, mood swings and unpredictability. He had trusted Channelize and opened himself up to her with some of his most inner and deepest secrets. Therefore, she knew she would need to handle Yanni with kid gloves. She owed him something, or so he thought, and he wasn't going to let her escape from him that easily. It was necessary and convenient for Channelize to distance herself from him, but they remained friends. There had also been rumours, floating around the grapevine, that Yanni was involved in narcotics and dealing. He had lost his job and needed extra money. Channelize didn't want to believe it. She hated drugs! They had destroyed her relationship with Paul, and managed to put her son behind bars. It certainly wasn't a path that Channelize wanted to go down, again.

VIVIEN'S REFLECTION

Vivien wasn't sure how she had managed to get home from her afternoon date with Channelize. She looked out of the window and she could see the yellow lights shining from each of the little, flat-roofed, Spanish houses. It was dark now. How long she had been sitting there in her arm chair, daydreaming? she wondered. Her wine glass was still tilted in her hand, half empty and warm. She could only assume that she had been sitting there, deep in thought, for a long time. Her thoughts were of Channelize. She was still reeling and saddened by the story of Fabergé. She had daughters of her own and could only imagine how hard and difficult a time it must have been for Channelize. She hadn't needed all the pettiness and gossip from the people in this town, thought Viv. She was still vulnerable and wounded. It wasn't without wonder, that Channelize had over reacted a few times. It all made sense to Viv, now.

Viv remembered how Channelize had been close to Lenny, a male friend of Herbert's. Viv had known him, too. However, Viv was more of a 'home bird' than Channelize. She didn't go out much in the evenings and preferred to just watch television indoors. However, Channelize was different. She seemed to hate her own company, and was always out in the bars every night. Viv often wondered where Channelize got the stamina. Lenny was a tall, elegant and charming man, in his sixties, but his age never stopped him from having a keen eye for the ladies. Channelize adored him. He was eccentric and amusing. They would sometimes role-play at flirting with each other, but it was always innocent and really harmless. Lenny enjoyed his drink, but would always try to advise Channelize of the pitfalls of alcohol. She regarded him more like a father figure. Channelize, could tell Lenny anything and he was sure to guard it with his life. He would never get involved in gossip of any kind.

At that time, Lenny had an ex-girlfriend, called Ramona, who used to teach Spanish lessons to the ex-pats. She was quite fluent in most languages, so one day Channelize asked Lenny if he could set up a meeting with her so that she could arrange some lessons. Of course, Lenny agreed. He thought it would be a great idea. However, a few days later, Channelize met up with Lenny in the Ice Bar. Viv recalled the surprise and hurt on Channelize's face by the response.

He told Channelize, as calmly and gently as he could, that Ramona blatantly refused. 'Why?" Channelize had asked, puzzled.

Lenny eyes looked down at the floor. It was difficult for him to say what came next… "Well, you may as well know…"

"Go on," urged Channelize, impatiently. #

He continued, "Her exact comments were, Channelize..."

he braced himself. "She didn't want a... negro... or words to that effect, in her house. I'm so sorry Channelize, my darling, it's not something I wanted to say however... it's the truth. And you might as well know how she really feels. If I were you, my darling, I would just ignore it, there're plenty of teachers around here," he said, sympathetically. But the damage was already done, he could see by the hurt in Channelize's eyes.

"Okay... Er, thanks, Lenny," Channelize replied. Feeling hurt and humiliated, she tried to force a smile and then turned to leave.

"Stay and have a drink with me, Chanel. I will tell you some funny jokes, that will cheer you up... come on, Channelize," Lenny shouted behind her.

"Maybe next time, Lenny," she replied, shouting over her shoulder.

Lenny felt angry and embarrassed by Ramona's attitude. He could hear the emotion in Channelize's voice. He shook his head in disgust as he sipped on his beer. He had always thought of Channelize like a daughter, and could never have dreamed of judging her in any other way.

Viv had been furious when Channelize had burst into her apartment on the verge of tears, and told her about the situation.

"It's not Lenny's fault," Channelize blurted,

protectively. "He was as horrified as I was, but he had to be honest with me… can you believe that, Viv?" she shrieked. "I feel like I have gone back in time. Is this the, Stone Age or Something? How dare she say such a stupid, ignorant comment about me, when she doesn't even know me as a person, Viv!"

Channelize ranted and raved, pacing up and down Viv's apartment. She flapped her hands in the air and pulled her fingers through her hair, as if she wanted to tear her hair out of every little follicle. She was in a flaming temper and Viv felt she needed to calm Channelize. Later that evening, after a few drinks, she knew Channelize would be gunning for Ramona.

"All right, I agree, it's a cruel and nasty thing to say about ya, but have you ever thought it might be outta jealousy? Viv replied.

Channelize, stopped pacing, she stood still to look at Viv, her hands rested firmly on her hips.

'What do you mean? Jealous of what? she replied, with a look of confusion.

'Well…" Viv continued, cautiously. "You do spend a lot of time with Lenny. I know, don't say it," she said, holding up the palms of her hands, as Channelize opened her mouth to interrupt.

"She's his ex-girlfriend, ain't she. Maybe, she saw you as some sort of threat. Or maybe, she thinks he's after you! After all, you know what an old flirt he is, don't cha?"

Channelize laughed. "That's ridiculous Viv! She

can't honestly think… that! Lenny's a lovely old chap but, more like a… well… a father. You know that, don't you?" She looked at Viv curiously.

Viv raised her eyebrows sceptically, "Yeah, course, I know that. But who knows what she's 'eard?"

Viv, continued to sit in her arm chair staring out at the night sky. It wouldn't have mattered what she had said to Channelize that day. Channelize was going to sort it out. And she did, just as Viv thought. After a few drinks in her system, she found, and confronted Ramona, and all hell had broken loose.

Viv sighed a deep sigh, placing both hands on her face and shaking her head. That type of nonsense was so typical around here and Channelize would always took the bait, she said to herself.

Channelize would always fight her own corner. She hated injustice of any kind, not just for herself but her friends and family, too. She had a good heart really, thought Viv. Minnie, her mother, now she was another kettle of fish. Viv had often witnessed Minnie demoralising Channelize. Viv felt it wasn't always done on purpose, but her insults and chastising toward Channelize, would destroy her. Minnie was the type of person with a venomous tongue once she was rattled. She would never support Channelize, and would automatically blame her for any wrong doing, without even knowing the other side of the story.

"It's that stupid Irish temper of yours. It's gonna land ya in a mountain o' trouble, Chanel, if you're not careful." Minnie would tell her. Viv, being a close friend, knew all that Channelize really wanted was to please her mother and receive even a fraction of praise. At that time, Channelize needed love and security from her mother, but it was never there. However, she had noticed that they had both grown closer since Herbert's illness.

Viv sat immersed in thought. How could she talk? She would hardly get the Perfect Mother Award, herself. She had tried to be there for both her daughters, offering them an unconditional love for as long as she could, because she could see how Channelize had been affected. Viv was beginning to feel tired now. She pulled her weary body up from the armchair. She felt so stiff and her old body ached. She slowly walked to the kitchen to make a cup of cocoa. Her head was throbbing now. All she wanted to do was have a wash and relax into her nice, comfortable bed. The kettle clicked off. It sounded like a bullet going off in Viv's head, "Why do I do this to myself? I know better than to get completely rat-arsed in the middle of the day. God, why do I do it to myself?" she muttered to herself, as she mixed up the hot cocoa.

Viv was drying her face and staring into the bathroom mirror. She realized the conversation with Channelize this afternoon, had really made her think about her own life and her girls. She was so lucky to have them and her grandchildren. She wanted to spend every minute with them and watch them grow up.

Something Channelize didn't, and wouldn't have the opportunity to do, with, Fabergé. Viv had been keeping a secret, too. She was ashamed that she hadn't shared it with her friend sooner, but maybe it hadn't been the best time, she thought.

Viv brushed her hair and pulled on her nightdress. She switched off the lights and got into bed. She slowly eased her head down onto her pillow. It was still a little fragile. She cursed herself again for drinking in the afternoon. She lay her head onto her plumped-up feather pillow, it felt comforting and cosy like a giant marshmallow.

"Ahaa," she sighed with relief. She lay there for a few minutes just staring at the ceiling. She had some pressing issues of her own on her mind, and she needed to make some serious decisions. But she was too tired to rack her brain any further tonight. She would need all her strength, to face what lay ahead of her.

12

Channelize was relieved to have opened up to Viv about Faberge. It had been the first time she had spoken about her for a long time and she was hoping that she could try to put the whole awful experience in a box. It had been four years, but she had always felt like it happened yesterday. She would never forget her little girl but, like Viv had said, 'it's not possible to bring her back'. She felt fortunate to have had Fabergé for three magic and memorable years, and she still had Brook, who very much needed her in his life. It had been devastating for Brook, too, losing his baby sister but, he had somehow managed to bottle up his feelings, preferring to support his mother in the only way a teenager could. He stood by helplessly, watching his mother barely surviving on medication and sleeping all day, every day. She hadn't meant to, however, she had closed Brook out of her life then, like she had closed everyone out. She had shut down and been beside herself with grief. It had been a long time ago, and Channelize felt the wounds would eventually heal.

The phone rang. Channelize rolled over to the other side of the bed to reach for the telephone,

"Hello," she answered sluggishly. The movement had caused her head to spin. A pounding ache whirled just above her left eye... Oh, God, she thought, when she realised she hadn't escaped the dreaded hangover. It was Darius,

"I take it you had a good day out with Vivien, then?" he asked,

"How did you know...?" Channelize questioned.

He interrupted her and said, "Don't ask... news travels fast around here. You should know that. I guess Vivien was her normal intoxicated self?" he said, presumingly. Channelize knew, Darius wasn't fond of Vivien. She remembered some bad blood between them in the past. It had been something to do with Gloria. She didn't really get involved. However, Viv had always been a good friend to Channelize.

"Why are you calling, I thought you would be at work?" she answered, choosing to ignore his last comment,

"I have a day off today. Would you like to go for a drive somewhere?" Channelize didn't have to think twice, she loved to get away from the town, and its prying eyes.

"Yes. That would be great, Darius!" she said.

"All right then. I will pick you up in half hour," he replied,

"Half hour!" exclaimed Channelize. "That doesn't give me much time."

But Darius wasn't having any of her excuses, "Half

93

hour," he repeated. "Half the day has gone already… see you later." And with that, he put the phone down.

Channelize jumped out of bed quickly, forgetting about the throbbing pain over her left eye. "Ooowch!" she cried. It felt like several almighty blows from a sledge hammer were repeatedly assaulting her brain. She looked at the time, it was eleven thirty. She headed for the bathroom cabinet to search for some desperately needed aspirin. She found the box, placed one tablet tentatively on the back of her tongue and then quickly washed it down with a gulp of tap water. She grimaced as she swallowed, she hated the taste of pills. Next, she jumped into the shower. It didn't really take her long to get ready. It was so hot, all she needed was her bikini, a pair of shorts, a light T-shirt, and her beach shoes. She bundled up a towel, a small bottle of water and some sun cream into her beach bag. She grabbed a cup of coffee and slice of toast, while she was on the move. Voila! she said to herself, she was ready. She checked the clock, it had just turned twelve. She was quite impressed with herself. Just at that moment, she heard the honking of a car horn outside. Darius was, once again, on time. Channelize quickly locked up the apartment and rushed out to meet him. His face was a golden brown and he looked fit and quite sexy, thought Channelize. She felt little butterflies of excitement, stir in her stomach. It had been a few days since they had seen each other. He leaned over and gave her a quick peck on the lips, instead of the normal traditional

Spanish kiss, cheek to cheek. Channelize looked surprised.

"You're in a good mood," she said with a smile. "I take it you're happy to see me?"

He looked her directly in the eyes, "Yeah... I've missed you. I was looking forward to us spending some time together. Just me and you. We will go over to a little island I know, on the south side. It's really pretty there." Channelize could hardly contain herself. The thought of spending a whole day with Darius, without feelings of guilt and other people judging them. What could be better?

They drove out to an idyllic spot. It was about half an hour's drive. Channelize had never been there before. She noticed a row of very grand, expensive Spanish villas, just overlooking a beautiful, long, sandy beach, with secluded little coves dotted here and there. The sea was transparent and glistened, as the sun bounced off each wave. There was a pretty Spanish tapas bar, perched high up on the cliff tops. They pulled up onto a gravelled car park which over looked a forest of lush palm trees. It was a scorching hot day, and Channelize couldn't wait to get into the sea and cool off.

They walked along the beach, enjoying the salty sea water washing over their feet. Darius spotted a cove with a handful of people sunbathing — others were reading quietly underneath the shade of their parasols. It was very tranquil. They found a shady spot which was protected from the sun by a large, jagged display of overhanging rock. Darius stripped down to his shorts and didn't wait a second before running towards the sea and throwing himself in.

"Come on!" he shouted to Channelize. "It's beautiful in here, and the waters really warm."

Channelize looked over to him and smiled as she laid all her necessities out on the sand and stripped down to her bikini. She ran toward Darius, acting like a hyperactive child, screaming and splashing about in the waves. The water was exhilarating and seemed to bring them both to life. They laughed, kissed and wrestled with the magnificent avalanche of waves covering them with foam, until eventually, they were both worn out. Darius held her hand as he pulled her out of the sea.

"Come on, hun. Let's relax and get some rays," he said. They both lay down on the towels, the sun beating down on their tanned skins. Channelize had to pinch herself, as she couldn't believe, lying next to her was a man she had only ever dared to dream about, but never imagined she would ever have, and here he was, lying right beside her. She wondered what he might be thinking as he lay there quietly, hidden behind his dark sunglasses? She decided it didn't really matter, she would just enjoy this wonderful day.

They both slept for about an hour. Darius had been in and out of the sea to cool off in between. Both of them were beginning to feel pangs of hunger and decided to pack up their belongings and head for the quaint little Spanish tapas bar perched on the cliff top. It was a nice, relaxing walk along the shore. Darius held Channelize's hand as they chatted about his relationship with Gloria, and the financial commitment they were both tied to, trying to sell the house. He ran a small construction business, which hadn't been very productive or viable, of late. His plans were to sell their house and cut all ties with Gloria. However, it didn't sound like it was going to be easy.

Channelize tried to change the subject. She felt embarrassed when he spoke like this. She didn't feel it was any of her business and today, of all days, she didn't want to think about Darius and his other life with Gloria. Maybe it was slightly selfish of her, she thought, but she hadn't felt this peaceful and content in a long time. She wanted their friendship to flourish and to concentrate on progressing with their relationship.

They finally reached the restaurant and noticed an empty table in a perfect spot situated on the terrace, near the railings, overlooking the sea. They sat down and within a few minutes the waiter appeared to take their order. They both opted for the, 'Garlic Mushrooms, Pork in Tomato and Pepper Sauce'. After the waiter had disappeared, Channelize noticed how quiet Darius had become, and observed him starring into the distance towards the sea, she waited a few moments and asked. "What's wrong?"

He looked at her vacantly, and replied, "I was just thinking how nice it would be to just... run away."

Channelize looked confused,

"Where would you run to?" she asked.

He pondered in thought for a while, and replied, "Just get as far away from this place and these people," he paused, his eyes fixed onto Channelize. "I want to be with you, Channelize, and now I can be, but not here. I want us to start afresh, somewhere where no one knows us."

Channelize knew that he was serious, because it was the first time he had admitted that he wanted something meaningful with her.

She relaxed back into her chair, folding her arms and mulling his thoughts around in her head. After all, neither of them really had anything to lose by moving on. Obviously, she would miss her mother and Amelia very much, but Vivien was still in a dilemma as to whether she would be staying in Spain. She leaned forward again, placing her elbows on the table and cupping her chin in her hands as she looked into his eyes...

"Well, it's something to think about," she replied. She didn't want to commit herself to anything just now, but it was a very tempting idea. Darius continued to stare out to sea.

"I have already thought about it, Channelize, and I am leaving, as soon as I can get some things tied up. I would really like you to come with me," he said, hesitantly.

Channelize's eyes widened, "You're really serious, aren't you?" she asked.

"Yes, never more so," he replied. Channelize thought deeply about his proposal. She turned her head to stare out to sea, half hoping and half expecting the sea would give her the answers. She knew she did not want to lose Darius, and she also knew that staying in Spain would be a lot worse, without him.

"All right then. Why not?" she replied impulsively, smiling from ear to ear, Darius smiled too. Channelize felt like a little girl, deciding whether to build a sandcastle or not? This was a big decision, but what the hell, what did either of them have to lose?

Darius leaned toward her attempting to kiss her lips, but his gesture was politely interrupted by the return of the waiter.

"Your tapas! Senior en Senorita."

"Er... gracia!" they replied in unison, looking slightly embarrassed. As the waiter walked away, Darius and Channelize both peeped over their sunglasses, mischievously, like two teenagers who had just been caught out having their first kiss. They both giggled as they tucked into their tapas.

13

As the weeks went on, Darius and Channelize grew stronger as a couple. They had become so comfortable in each other's company and Darius was working hard to try to find the finances to start a new life elsewhere. It made more sense to both of them for Darius to move into Channelize's apartment. Gloria had moved out of the house and was living with her new partner. It was the perfect opportunity for Darius to find new tenants to bring in another income. Meanwhile, times were getting harder for Channelize at work. Her hours had been reduced to two or three days a week, in a local bar called Trio's. The bar had been so quiet recently and customers were few and far between. Channelize would occupy her time by cleaning the terrace, stock-taking and refilling the large soda fridges, over and over again. There had been talk by the other staff members that Maggie, the owner, was thinking of closing down, too. There were a number of businesses closing down at that time, and unfortunately, Darius was no exception.

One evening he came home from work looking grave and disappointed.

"There's no more contracts, Channelize. Work is finished for me here. There's nothing left. It's all finished," he said, complacently.

Channelize looked shocked. She knew the situation was dire, but Darius had always been able to turn his hand to anything and he was very well known in the ex-pat community. He had never before had a problem finding work. He had no alternative but to go through the process of releasing all his employees.

During dinner that evening, Darius mentioned that he had a brother living in France. He had spoken to him on the telephone earlier in the day and he was rather excited about the news his brother, Simon, had told him.

"Apparently, Channelize, there's plenty of work in France in the area where Simon is living. He said that he could help me get started. He has masses of work ongoing and actually needs extra help! What do you think?" he asked, excitedly.

Channelize hadn't seen Darius look so motivated about anything in a long time, but it she thought it all seemed a bit too good to be true, especially since every part of Europe and the world were suffering this terrible recession. However, it would be nice to start afresh with Darius. The tongues had already been wagging about the two of them 'shacking up together', or so she had heard.

"Well, I guess it would be worth a try. Why don't you look into it a little further?" she replied.

They spent most of that evening talking it over and working out the pros and cons of moving to France. Admittedly, there seemed to be more pros than cons.

Finally, they decided it would be a good idea to travel to France for a ten-day visit, to see how they both felt about it. Darius, had been there before and always raved about the place, but it was a big move for Channelize and she couldn't afford to make any rash decisions. They phoned Simon later that evening. He was more than happy for them to visit. Channelize couldn't wait to tell Amelia and Vivien the news, but she was slightly concerned about how her mother would take it.

The next day, Channelize arranged to meet Amelia for their weekly 'ladies do lunch' day.

They arranged to meet around two o clock in the afternoon at Angelo's. As usual, Amelia was late, so by the time she arrived Channelize was bursting to tell her the news. Amelia listened patiently, waiting for Channelize to come up for air.

"Have you finished?" she smiled, leaning back into her chair. "Right! Shall I tell you what I think, now?" she asked.

Channelize looked intrigued. she thought Amelia would have been more excited for her.

Amelia continued. "Channelize, don't you think it's a big move, especially with Darius? You haven't been together that long and it's a whole new country, a new language to learn. Do you really think your relationship is strong enough? He could still be on the rebound from Gloria." Channelize felt deflated and hurt by Amelia's honesty, which Amelia sensed. She leaned across the table and took hold of Channelize's hand.

"Look, I'm your best friend and really don't wish to burst your bubble, but it's a big move and if anything went wrong with your relationship, you wouldn't have anyone to turn to. Not me, or your mother. Maybe you should think about this a little more, Channelize. You're putting an awful lot of trust in Darius."

Channelize felt disappointed. It wasn't quite the reaction she had been expecting or hoping for from Amelia, but she couldn't help thinking that maybe she was right. Maybe she was jumping in feet first or — maybe not? After thinking for a few minutes, she responded.

"Amelia, how do you know who is right or wrong for you?" she protested. Life is a gamble. Besides, me and Darius are both in the same place in our lives at the moment and remember, I have known Darius as a friend for a long time. I think I can trust him as far as any other man and now we are lovers. Well, I think I know him… slightly better." Channelize blushed, shyly.

"Yeah, I'm sure you do!" interrupted Amelia teasingly.

They continued to analyse the situation for most of the afternoon, as they often used to about everything. Channelize knew Amelia only had her best interest at heart.

They conversed about other interesting developments taking place. Ruby, Amelia's mother, was coming to Spain for a visit and a much-needed holiday. She would be meeting Yusef for the first time.

Ruby had only ever known Amelia's ex-husband, Ryan, and Channelize got the impression that Amelia was feeling slightly apprehensive about introducing Ruby to the new man in her life. Yusef was Moroccan, a completely different culture and a completely different person to Ryan.

By the end of the afternoon's discussions, Channelize and Amelia had both concluded that a ten-day visit to France would be the best option, instead of just uprooting altogether. Amelia had known just how unhappy and depressed Channelize had become with all of the gossip going around. Amelia had always made a point of not allowing herself to get too involved with the ex-pats, while she had been living in Spain. She protected herself and Yusef from the gossip by keeping herself isolated. She had often said to Channelize,

"I don't understand how you cope with all the nonsense they say about you. You must be pretty thick-skinned, Channelize?" But the insults and insinuations did effect Channelize, grinding her down, little by little, though she would never express those feelings to Amelia. She would hide her pain, normally through getting rotten drunk. However, her behaviour would only cause more room for gossip.

"There's that tramp from last night," she would hear them whispering, as she walked past. "She made a right show of herself last night. I mean, goodness me, how could you let yourself get in such a state? Tsk tsk."

14

Channelize would walk by and smile. Naturally, the 'clucking hens', which is how she referred to them now, would smile back at her. They were so two-faced, Channelize would think to herself. She just wanted some peace and a normal life with someone she loved. Amelia understood, and in the end, she wished her well. Just before she left Angelo's bar, Amelia turned to Channelize with a tear in her eye.

"Actually, I'm being selfish. I just don't want you to go. I hope you hate France!" she said, stamping her feet in a child-like tantrum. "I can't imagine life here, without my best friend." They both smiled, Amelia was so special to her, too. She had been her life saver for the past eighteen months, and she had kept Channelize grounded. They had so much fun together. It would be heart-breaking to leave Amelia and Minnie behind, she thought to herself. Channelize felt dejected and confused. She hugged Amelia tightly as they said their goodbyes and went their separate ways.

It was late afternoon as Channelize walked along the street towards her apartment. In the distance, she could see the heat oscillating from the tarmac off the road. It was desperately hot. She was aware of the quiet stillness of the empty streets. It was similar to a ghost town at this time of day. All the Spaniards had the sense to stay indoors and take their siesta. Channelize watched as a rather emancipated stray dog tried to salvage some old scraps of food from an overloaded dustbin. A few yards behind him, was a poor, dishevelled hobo pushing a supermarket trolley filled with broken bits of furniture that had been retrieved from a skip.

Her heart went out to him. He appeared dirty and thin, it was obvious that he hadn't washed or eaten a healthy meal in weeks. Channelize felt ashamed, as she watched both of them. He was no better off than the stray dog, she thought, they were both just trying to survive. And this was supposed to be paradise.

She walked further along the street. Her eyes fixed admiringly on the elite and expensive houses equipped with several bedrooms, Olympic-size swimming pools and top-of-the-range sports cars, parked in their tiled driveways. These houses were mostly used as holiday homes, occupied two, or maybe three times a year. And here, right in front of her eyes was the other end of the spectrum. A human being scavenging to find a leftover meal from a bin. How unfair, she thought, as she watched and wondered how this poor hobo's life had become so bad. What had gone so wrong? Things were not quite that bad for Channelize yet. However, she couldn't help think to herself, there, but for the grace of God, go I. There had to be more to life than this, Channelize thought, sadly. There had to be a better life… somewhere.

Channelize, strolled leisurely home. She wanted to think clearly about her circumstances and mull over the things she had talked about with Amelia. Before she was aware of it, she was outside Viv's apartment block. I wonder if she's home? she thought to herself, as she found herself crossing the road and pressing Viv's buzzer. It was quickly answered by Viv.

"Hello, who is it?" Viv asked.

"It's only me, Viv, are you busy?" replied Channelize.

"No babe. I've always got time for a tea break. Come on up."

Channelize entered the building and made her way slowly up the stairs. The afternoon heat had tired her out, she was feeling quite depressed with herself and drained. She hadn't spent much time with Viv since her last day off work, apart from fleeting exchanges in the supermarket, and a lot had happened since then. She wanted to get Viv's thoughts on the 'French connection'. Viv had always been honest with her in the past and Channelize respected her opinion. The back door to Viv's apartment was already open and Channelize found Viv sitting on the sofa, watching the television. By her side was an opened letter. She looked up at Channelize and forced a smile. Channelize noticed her eyes looked puffy and red through her spectacles.

"Hi babe, wanna cuppa? I will put the kettle on." As she moved past Channelize towards the kitchen, Viv peered at Channelize over her glasses. "Oh dear, babe, looks like you lost a dollar and found a dime. What's rattling you?" she asked.

Channelize sat down on the sofa and replied glumly, "Oh, everything and nothing."

Viv prepared the cups, milk and sugar and peered again over her glasses. "Well, what's that supposed to mean? Tell your Auntie Viv," she smiled comfortingly at Channelize. They sat down together and Channelize told her the whole scenario about Darius and the opportunity in France, Amelia's opinion on the matter and her feelings regarding leaving her mother, with Herbert being so sick. Vivien listened intently, as Channelize poured her heart out.

"Well, if you're asking for my opinion? First and foremost, it's your life Channelize. You already know my feelings about Darius, and to be honest, I probably wouldn't trust him as far as I could throw him, but saying that, I don't trust any bloody man!" she laughed, and Channelize giggled, too. "Go for it, babe! See how you feel after the ten-day visit, and then make your mind up."

Channelize kissed Viv on the cheek and smiled. "You always make things sound so simple, Viv," she said.

At that point Vivien lowered her head and a tear fell from her eyes.

"What's wrong... what's happened?" Channelize asked.

Vivien picked up the letter from the sofa. "Read this," she said quietly, handing the letter to Channelize. As she read the black print, Channelize's eyes widened. Halfway down the page she saw the word, cancer, it sprang out like a cobra, from the page. She tried to read further, however, she had only absorbed one word. She stared at Vivien, overwhelmed with concern.

"When did this come?" asked Channelize, not really knowing what to say.

"Oh, a few days ago," Viv responded.

"Why didn't you tell me?" proclaimed Channelize. "Instead of letting me waffle on about my problems. Is it... serious?" Channelize asked, looking at Viv, her eyes full of compassion. Viv, stood up lethargically and turned to face the window. She was silent for a few moments.

"I don't know yet, babe. I have to go back to England for some tests, what kind of tests, I'm not sure yet." She turned around to face Channelize. "Well, at least I will get to see my little grandchildren. Maybe it was fate or something, hey Channelize? I was thinking about going back home, and now I have no choice so... that's sorted then, ain't it?" she said, half-heartedly.

They continued to discuss Vivien's plans and her cancer. Channelize sensed that underneath her bravado, Vivien was actually petrified — not for herself, she never thought of herself — but for her children and not seeing her girls and her grandchildren growing up.

Vivien had decided to get a flight back to England

at the end of that week. The hospital was to start the dreaded tests at the end of the following week, so she would be able to spend some quality time with her family beforehand. Channelize was glad Viv was going so quickly. She would miss her terribly but she knew the sooner they started the treatment on Viv, the better her chances of a full recovery. Viv opened a bottle of red wine. They sat outside on the balcony together, enjoying a few laughs and reminiscing over past events.

"So, you see, Channelize, life's too short to waste time," Viv slurred, as she poured her third glass. "Sometimes, choices come along and choose you, without you even having to make any choices for yourself."

That was the last time Viv and Channelize were in each other's company, and those were the last words Channelize remembered.

At the end of that week, Vivien flew back to England. She kept in touch with Channelize for a while. She had managed to find a job working a few hours a day, she had met new friends and rekindled old friendships. During their telephone conversation, Channelize could tell in Viv's voice that she sounded much happier being back around her family and what she called normality. The radiotherapy treatment Vivien was undergoing, seemed to be working well. However, it was continuous and Viv would often be too tired to speak on the telephone for long periods. Channelize tried to call her as often as she could, whilst life went on in this little Spanish town… without her.

A new Russian bar was opening in the town. Darius and Channelize had decided to attend the opening night. Money was still very tight for the two of them. However, Darius had recently completed a decorating job and had a few other small, odd jobs lined up so they decided they could afford to splash out a little.

"Why don't we go to the new bar tonight?" Darius had asked. He certainly didn't have to ask Channelize twice. She hadn't been out socialising for ages and was dressed and ready to go in no time at all.

When Channelize and Darius arrived, they were greeted by the proprietors. They were a young couple from Russia in their mid-thirties. They were friendly and welcoming and had laid on an impressive barbecue buffet for the occasion. The food was delicious and Channelize couldn't help but compliment the owner, Vladimir, for the array of delicious Russian salad dishes.

"The food is excellent, and the place looks amazing!" Channelize remarked.

"Oh, I glad you like," he replied. "Excuse my English, my wife is much better," he replied, apologetically. Channelize smiled.

"No problem," she said, dismissing Vladimir with her hand. "You should hear my Russian!"

He looked at her slightly vaguely and then made his excuses to mingle. Darius looked at Channelize, amused. "Well, that went down like a lead balloon," he said, looking at Channelize. She raised her eyebrows and shrugged her shoulders flippantly.

"Maybe he doesn't understand the English sense of humour?" she replied.

"Your sense of humour, don't you mean?" replied Darius sarcastically, they both smiled and giggled at one another. Steadily, people started to arrive and Vladimir walked over to greet each one of them warmly. Channelize observed that Vladimir seemed like a genuine and sincere person. He obviously didn't realise that most of the ex-pats were just looking for a free meal, and would probably never support his bar again, she thought, cynically. However, the evening began to slowly liven up. Vladimir and his wife Nadia had also organised a Spanish guitar player to add to the atmosphere. All of the guests were dancing and enjoying themselves, the alcohol flowed freely and the ambiance was relaxed and friendly. As Channelize chatted away to Darius, he commented on her glass being empty. "Oh! we can't have that now, can we?" he said boisterously. "I won't be a second. I'm just going to the bar. Another wine, darling?" he said sarcastically.

"Err... maybe a strawberry milk shake?" she replied, humorously. He smiled and headed off towards the bar. Channelize stood there for a while in her own little world, appreciating the decor and the changes the Russian couple had made to the place. She caught sight of her image in the glass doorway and admired her white flowing strapless dress, which she hadn't had a chance to wear in a while. She felt very feminine, cool and sexy, with her hair tied up in a French plait. Whilst she was engrossed in flattering her own ego in the mirrored door, she noticed a man walking towards the glass doorway.

"Oh no!" she thought, instantly. It was Yanni. He looked stoned, either from drug or alcohol abuse, Channelize wasn't sure. However, he had that look on his face, which she was very familiar with. That look, that he portrayed when he felt the whole world was out to get him. He had obviously wound himself up about something. It had filtered through the grapevine that he was jealous of Channelize being with Darius. And here he was, walking in to the same room as both of them, with that look. Channelize's eyes followed him intently, as he headed toward the bar.

15

Darius had just turned to walk away from the counter, as Yanni approached. Yanni pushed by Darius on purpose, causing the wine to splatter all over the arm his shirt.

"Hey, watch it!" Darius said, as he walked toward Channelize.

"What an idiot," he said, handing Channelize her wine and trying to dry himself off with a serviette. "I'm sure he did that on purpose," Darius said, staring at Yanni with a look of contempt. Channelize just shrugged her shoulders. After the obvious confrontation between Yanni and Darius, Channelize felt uncomfortable. She was monitoring Yanni and his behaviour from the corner of her eye and could see that he was also disturbing other people on purpose, and generally becoming more obnoxious. She watched him fuelling himself with shots of whiskey, as if they were going out of fashion. It was getting late, anyway, and Channelize suggested to Darius that they leave. The bar was beginning to empty out and it seemed appropriate, Darius was also quite intoxicated by that time, too. They said their goodbyes to Vladimir and Nadia, and a few of the other familiar faces, who were hovering around for the final call on drinks. They left.

The apartment was only five minutes from the Russian bar. However, because Darius was so intoxicated and unsteady on his feet, he struggled along at a snail's pace, which frustrated Channelize. It seemed to be taking forever to get home. Finally, Channelize was relieved to see the gated entrance to their apartment. For a moment, she thought her eyes were playing tricks on her, when she spotted a small red glow and someone lurking outside the gate. It appeared to be the silhouette of a person, a male figure, in the darkness. Her eyes suddenly widened as she got closer. She realised the figure was Yanni. He was leaning on the wall, smoking a cigarette. Darius was babbling about something and was totally oblivious.

"Darius," whispered Channelize. "Yanni is waiting for us at the gate, oh my God, what's he up to?" Channelize said, suspiciously.

"What! What's he doing there, that idiot," bumbled Darius in a drunken slur. "He knocked my drink on me on purpose, Channelize, did you see that?" he proclaimed, loudly and indignantly. He pointed his finger at Yanni accusingly and tried hard to focus. "What an idiot" protested Darius, raising his voice again.

"Shush… keep your voice down, and pull yourself together," Channelize said angrily, grabbing Darius by the arm and trying to straighten him up. "He can be a very dangerous person when he is like this," she persisted.

"Oh, yeah. He's that crazy ex-boyfriend of yours, isn't he? Well, you should know!" Darius said scornfully, and roared with laughter. "I will protect you, honey, from the big, bad, bogey man," he said, leaning heavily on Channelize's shoulder, and whispering annoyingly in her ear. Channelize eased his arm off her shoulder. She was getting more frustrated with his antics.

"God, Darius. You are such an idiot sometimes!" she snapped.

As they both approached the gate, Channelize came face to face with Yanni. He had a smug look on his face. She felt the force of his eyes burning through her. He stared threateningly at her and then turned his gaze on Darius.

'This is what you want? This type of person, he is not even a man. Look at him, he is a fool!" he stated, spitting on Darius's shoes.

"Listen, Yanni, we don't want any trouble. We have all had a bit too much to drink. Let's just call it a night, and go home," Channelize said, appealing to Yanni's better nature, and trying desperately, to hide the fact that her legs were trembling.

"Who, are you calling a fool?" Darius replied, suddenly alerted. Channelize pleaded with Darius to come inside and keep quiet but he wasn't having any of it. He struggled with Channelize as she tried to pull him by the arm in her direction. It was impossible. Darius started to shout insults at Yanni. The situation became highly charged as Yanni began to bite his bottom lip with anger. He inhaled heavily, adjusting his stance, ready for battle, his eyes still transfixed on Darius. Channelize was beginning to feel panic. The pushing and shoving started between the two men and before she knew it, fists were flying. Darius was finding it hard to keep his balance and fell onto the ground. However, this did not stop Yanni.

He continued to kick Darius brutally in the stomach and ribs, shouting abusive language in Spanish.

"Stop it, stop!" cried Channelize, grabbing at Yanni's clothing and trying to pull him away. He turned and pushed her down onto the ground, discarding her like a rancid piece of meat. The tears welled up inside Channelize. She could see that Darius was at a disadvantage and was taking a terrible beating from Yanni. It suddenly dawned on her that she had her mobile phone in her handbag. She tried desperately to retrieve it and eventually, within few seconds, she found it. She dialled 116, the emergency services number for the police, but just as she heard a voice say, "Ola, policia," she was disconnected. The phone was snatched from her hand. She felt her thumb bone crack with the force. Yanni called her a "putta!" which Channelize understood as, bitch and then threw the phone along the road until it smashed into small pieces.

Channelize was shocked, afraid and in pain. She didn't recognise Yanni at this stage, he was crazy and out of his mind with rage. Darius had managed to drag himself up from the ground. He threw his arms around Yanni's neck and held him tightly in a choke-hold. Channelize's blood ran cold, as she watched Yanni pull a flick knife from his pocket. He was struggling to unravel Darius's arms from around his throat. Somehow, they both fell backwards onto the pavement, Darius was underneath Yanni, still holding on for dear life. They wrestled around on the ground. Channelize was yelling and screaming for someone to help. She could see, in the distance, two people running toward her.

"Help, help!" she shouted louder, waving her hands frantically to attract their attention.

She turned around to see what was happening between the two men. She watched in horror as Yanni, slowly and methodically, lifted his body up from the ground. He was looking down at Darius, whose body was still and lifeless. Yanni looked terrified. He stared longingly, at Channelize. This time, without hate in his eyes, but fear! He opened his mouth to say something, but his words were paralysed.

"What have you done, Yanni? Why, have you done this?" Channelize whispered, quietly. Yanni paused for a second, looking helplessly at Channelize. His eyes were glazed with tears and urging her for forgiveness. Then, as agile as a cat which had just finished devouring its prey, he turned and ran off into the darkness. There was a deathly silence.

At that point, two men arrived at the scene. Channelize remembered seeing them in the Russian bar. She was familiar with one of them, he was Spanish, and his name was Sebastian. The other man was English, he was on holiday. Sebastian called him Rob. They both bent down to try to assist Darius to his feet. He wasn't moving. However, he was breathing. The men looked at each other gravely. As they rolled Darius gently onto his back, Sebastian noticed blood on his fingers. Channelize was hovering over them in a state of shock. She vaguely heard Sebastian's voice say to Rob, "It looks like he's been stabbed. Call an ambulance, quickly!"

The next moment, Channelize found herself sitting in a hospital waiting room. It was five a.m. and Darius had been whisked off for surgery. She sat there alone, staring at the sparse, white walls. Her elegant white dress was now filthy and blood-stained, from nursing Darius, while she had waited for the ambulance to arrive. He had been delusional and barely coherent, the blood still oozing through his shirt. She hadn't spoken to anyone. It would be too early in the morning to call her mother or Amelia. She desperately needed to hear some reassuring words, then she remembered her mobile was smashed to pieces, somewhere. She began to relive the nightmare in her thoughts.

She remembered herself and Darius enjoying a nice evening, up until the point where Yanni decided to destroy it, and this was the outcome. This was where

Channelize had found herself. Sitting in a Spanish hospital waiting room, whilst Darius, the man she loved, lay in the intensive care unit. She was filled with remorse, not knowing if Darius would live or die. At that moment she felt nothing for Yanni, other than hate and repulsion. Look what he had done, she thought, and for what? Pure jealousy and control. She wished she had never met Yanni. She wished he was the one lying in that hospital bed, fighting for his life. She covered her eyes and started to cry as her thoughts drifted back to Darius. What if he died? It would be all her fault, she would blame herself forever and the whole town would blame her. Channelize wiped her eyes on her tattered dress. She knew that if they stayed in Spain, neither she or Darius would have any peace from Yanni. The story would spread like wildfire and by tomorrow, everyone would be thinking that she had stabbed Darius and no doubt there would be a whole new spin on it. She was hated enough in this town by the ex-pats. Some of them had warned him not to get involved with Channelize, but he hadn't listened. "Why hadn't he listened?" she said angrily to herself. She was so mixed up, but one thing was for sure, if Darius survived, they would both be better off starting a new life in France.

The doctor suddenly appeared, holding a clipboard. He was Spanish, but he spoke very good English. He gave Channelize a broad smile as he approached her.

"At least it's good news," he said. Darius was doing well. Channelize sighed with relief. He told Channelize, they had given him a blood transfusion. Apparently, one of his lungs had been punctured. He would need to stay in the hospital for a while longer. "He's not out of the woods yet," the doctor added, with an air of uncertainty. "A lot depends on the next few days when we can evaluate exactly how much internal damage had been done."

It still sounded very serious to Channelize. The doctor advised her to make a report to the police, "So they could find and arrest the culprit who has done this," he said, sternly.

"Are you hurt in any way?" he asked, as he took a minute to glance down at Channelize's dress.

"No, not really. I just have a little pain, here" she replied, as she pointed to her thumb.

She had a few cuts and bruises on her arms and knees, but her thumb and part of her hand were now a purple-blue colour, and bent at an awkward angle. It was impossible to move. The doctor examined it.

"All right then, we had better get someone to look at that for you." He smiled broadly again, turned and walked away. Channelize was still trying to take in everything the doctor had said. She felt sick to her stomach. She hoped and prayed that Darius would pull through. The next few days would be crucial.

16

Ten days later, Darius was released from hospital. He hadn't completely recovered and was still a little fragile and bruised. Fortunately, all of his internal organs were functioning normally. After a few weeks of tender loving care and gentle physiotherapy from Channelize, Darius was strong enough to get back on his feet again. The only indication of his wound, was a small scar on the left-hand side of his torso. They had discussed whether they should press charges against Yanni. However, the whole ordeal for Darius had taken its toll mentally and physically. He had decided they had both suffered enough stress and grief from Yanni. All Darius wanted to do was move on with their plans. The Spanish police, however, required a statement concerning that dreadful evening and eventually accepted Darius and Channelize's version of events. They reluctantly told him, they had been mugged by a stranger, who had jumped out behind them as they approached the gate. Channelize explained, that it had been too dark to get a clear description of his face? The police officer seemed convinced, due to the increased crime rate, which had been escalating out of control recently. He scribbled down the details on his notepad, whilst nodding his head sympathetically.

"You are a lucky one, amigo," he said, in his broken English, before affectionately tapping Darius on the shoulder. He headed towards the kitchen door as Channelize followed him.

"Gracias, senor," she said.

The policeman turned to face her. "It might be wise to put a security light out here, Senorita." he said, pointing to an ideal spot overlooking the gate. "Next time, your friend… he's not so lucky."

"Si, si, I will," replied Channelize. She lingered at the doorway as the officer made his way across the terrace to the gate. Her eyes fixed on the recommended spot above the gate.

She felt guilty. She tried not to make eye contact with the officer. He opened the gate to leave. She hated lying, especially to the police and she wasn't very good at it either.

"Adios, senorita," he called out.

"Oh, err… Adios," replied Channelize uncomfortably, closing the gate behind him.

Darius was at last, fit enough to drive the long journey to France. They had already finalised the details with Penny and Simon. It was the perfect time to escape to a change of scenery. Channelize had spoken to her mother after the attack on Darius. She had been shocked and disappointed that Yanni could do such a despicable thing and she wholeheartedly supported their decision to investigate a new lifestyle in France. So, with everyone's blessing, Darius and Channelize drove the thirteen-hour trip to France. It was a long and tiring journey. However, the mind-blowing views of the rolling mountains and breath-taking landscape en route, occupied Channelize throughout the lengthy journey. They had stopped intermittently to refuel and stretch their cramped legs. However, they had been travelling for thirteen hours and were both exhausted and relieved to finally reach Simon and Penny's house at around eleven o'clock, that evening. Both Simon and Penny had waited up to greet them at the doorway. Simon was a tall man with a rugged, friendly face, spiky hair and prominent, round eyes. Penny was slightly shorter than Simon, with straight, brown hair. She was wrapped in a thick, black cardigan and wore a three-quarter-length corduroy skirt, with flat leather boots. She appeared younger than Simon. She had a peach complexion and a broad smile. They ushered Darius and Channelize up a stone spiral staircase, which led to a spacious living room on the first floor. Channelize immediately felt the chill of the cool temperature on her skin. The climate was colder in France, she thought to herself, compared to what she was used to. She was glad that she had packed at least two heavy sweaters for herself and Darius. The living room was tastefully decorated with a large wine-coloured sofa with thick, padded cushions. A marble, unlit fire place appeared to be the centre piece of the room. The house itself was a three-storey, old French town house, which echoed traditional French character. Smart wooden timber frames surrounded each window, replacing the original old ones. It was apparent to Channelize, that Simon had started various refurbishing projects around the house to enhance its former glory. Brand new French doors opened out onto an impressive-sized garden filled with trees and shrubs. Channelize couldn't really appreciate the beauty of it, until the next morning. Penny and Simon said that it wasn't cold enough yet to need the heaters on. Channelize looked wryly, at Darius.

"You will get used to it," Simon said amused, as he observed Channelize's expression. "Maybe, it's because you are so used to the climate in Spain. The nights are chilly, but its warmer in the daytime." Channelize wasn't convinced. Penny had prepared a small meal of mince and potatoes. Channelize and Darius tucked in, gratefully. They chatted briefly about their journey and life in Spain, then all four of them retired to bed.

The next morning, the sun was shining. "Seems like Simon was right," Channelize said, turning her gaze from the window. It was unusual for Darius to still be in bed at eleven o'clock in the morning, but he was so exhausted from the drive. He started to stir. "It's a beautiful day, Darius, let's get out!" Channelize said, leaping on top of him.

They decided to take a long walk around the city to find out more about their new surroundings. The city appeared completely different in the daylight compared to the stillness of the previous evening, when they had arrived. Channelize was amazed and pleasantly surprised at how busy and active the streets were. A French market had set up its stalls. There were all different types of people and nationalities filling their large wicker baskets to the brim with fresh fruit and vegetables. As Darius and Channelize slowly mingled with the crowd, they both felt a tinge of excitement, as they listened to the dulcet tones of the French people conversing. It was a beautiful language and sounded more like people singing rather than speaking, thought Channelize. It was a gentle, romantic accent and Channelize couldn't wait to start learning French.

The long streets were lined with birch trees. With the onset of winter, a few had begun to shed their leaves. Her eyes widened at the sight of parks and colourful cartoon-figured play areas for the children and thick green grass outlined with neat floral arrangement everywhere. Channelize was overwhelmed at the amount of natural greenery here in France — it reminded her so much of England. This was the Languedoc region, and a complete contrast to the area of Spain they had come from. It was humid and baron in the Spanish coastal towns, hardly any lush green areas like France. The air here felt different, fresh and oxygenated, thought Channelize. She noticed the traditional French architectural buildings all around her. The oblong French windows were a predominant feature of every house and apartment, accompanied by sturdy, thick, wooden shutters. These heavy wooden doors had obviously given valiant service during the Second World War, thought Channelize. She could almost hear the banging of the German battering rams trying to invade these classic French homes. However, they had stood the test of time and were complimented by elegant, French-styled balcony railings. Most of the houses in the city were tall, three-storey buildings, thin ones and fat ones stood side by side, each with its own individual personality. They were huddled together on spotlessly clean streets, adorned with trees, that resembled a long line of French soldiers, all standing to attention. There were artistically designed water fountains situated around the city, with cherub statues tilting small ceramic pots, cascading flows of water. The centre of the city was bustling, a melting pot of all kinds of people, from new-age drop-outs, eccentric types, mixed race and mixed-gender couples, students and professionals. The rich and affluent Madames delicately tottered along in their designer shoes and wafted expensive Cristian Dior perfume. Clutched helplessly underneath their arms, were tiny pooch accessories. The Monsieurs oozed a mixture of distinction, sophistication and wealth. People of all walks of life lived here. Artistic creativity and different cultures all existed together, within a civilized and relaxed atmosphere. Channelize felt the people here held a respect for one another's lifestyle, devoid of judgment. She was fascinated, as she hadn't witnessed an open-minded attitude like this, in a long time.

Darius and Channelize spent the whole day touring around 'la cite'. The place was diverse, with everything it had to offer. Channelize compared the old buildings to her grandmother — old, warm and friendly. The ancient buildings exuded a tired and almost worn-out exterior. However, she couldn't help but feel transfixed by their life and sheer character. Channelize thought to herself, if only their walls could speak. She could only imagine the interesting and endless stories they would tell. It was obvious to Channelize that these 'old ladies' were once the beauty queens of their time. They had weathered over the years, which had only added to their stunning beauty and grace.

The, Central Plaza was a meeting point where the French people would sit, whiling away the hours, drinking coffee, wine, and indulging themselves in lengthy lunch breaks. Channelize especially enjoyed listening to the French language and the vibrant conversations of the young students who sat beside them. The Plaza was also a central area for a variety of expensive shops and boutiques. As Channelize looked eagerly at the chocolate and pastry designs displayed in the windows of the patisseries. She couldn't help admire the works of art.

"It would almost be a crime to eat them," she said to Darius.

The Central Plaza was filled with art galleries, lingerie shops, beauty salons, perfumeries and crepe stalls on every corner. The air was alive with all the different smells. Darius and Channelize were completely wrapped up in the whole ambiance of the place. The assistants in the shops were especially polite and friendly and tried very hard to be as helpful as possible, considering the language barrier. Channelize and Darius explored each cobbled street surrounding the city. They enjoyed pottering around the quaint boutiques and antique shops. Darius had compared all the little cobbled alleyways to rabbit runs, which burrowed through the city, only to reveal a different vista and new perception of it once you reached the end.

Channelize agreed and said philosophically,

"Yep, it's similar to life really, Darius. We never know where each individual path will lead us or what we will find at the other end."

They smiled at each other warmly, clasping each other's hand, whilst thinking about their own ironic situation.

The weather had been beautiful and Channelize had already decided that France with Darius, was exactly where she wanted to be.

They spent the rest of their ten-day break, exploring the outskirts of the city. They came across a huge lake, which catered to all types of summer and winter activities. A man-made, sandy beach was encased in an idyllic setting, the view was breath-taking. People jogged and cycled, children played bat-and-ball games. It was such a refreshing change for Channelize to see people participating in outdoor sports, rather than just sitting in Angelo's bar, growing old and boring. With hindsight, she suddenly realised that was exactly what she had been doing herself. She had always been an active and sporty person, however, she had changed her lifestyle so much since she had been living in Spain. The coastal beaches were close by, too. Simon had told them of a beach only twenty minutes' drive away.

'It does get very hot here in the summer months, even though it's green like England, we usually do get a longer and hotter summer," Simon had said. He had also assured Darius about the employment situation, too, offering him work for a good eight months.

Channelize and Darius were so excited about the move they could hardly wait for the ten days to end, so they could get back to Spain and start packing!

17

During their time in France, Channelize and Darius had made some enquiries, about renting a property. Simon and Penny had invited them to stay for as long as they needed to. However, Channelize felt that it wouldn't be a suitable arrangement, long term. They devoted the last few days of their holiday, to surfing several of the popular estate agencies, which Penny had told them about. Disappointed and disheartened, they soon came to realise that many of the agencies required certain documents, which they didn't have with them, and also massive administration fees for their services, which they didn't have either. Channelize had begun to feel quite despondent by the end of the day. They would need a place of their own to store all their furniture and personal items which they would be bringing from Spain?

"Oh well! I guess that's it, then," Channelize whined to Darius. She sat down on a bench removing her boots and rubbing her feet, which were burning from walking for hours. Channelize could see her dream of living in France, fading away in front of her eyes. "What can we do now?" she said, wearily.

Darius tried to stay positive and light hearted.

"Well, you could always sell your body to make some money," he replied, teasingly. Channelize stared at him dryly and rolled her eyes.

"That's not even funny, Darius!" she proclaimed, and lowered her head in defeat.

He walked over to her and put his arm around her shoulders, kissing her tenderly on the cheek. "I'm sorry," he replied, smiling. "Something will come up, it always does. Do you remember when I was worrying about getting tenants for my house to help pay the mortgage and then suddenly, in the nick of time, they turned up?" Channelize looked up at him with doe eyes and nodded. "Then, trust me Channelize. If it's meant to be, it will be." Darius said, optimistically. "Come on, Channelize, let's go and get something to eat, I'm starving."

They had both become much closer since the attack on Darius. Channelize felt lucky and very grateful to still have him around. Both of them desperately needed a fresh start where they would not be the object of gossip, a place where they could concentrate on strengthening their relationship. Channelize had been so excited about the move and the prospect of meeting new and interesting people, who had more to talk about than the toiletry habits of the neighbour's cat, or, who in the town had just drunk themselves into an early grave. Channelize was tired of the bigoted and pompous attitude of some of the ex-pats. Visiting France had been such a refreshing change from all of it. No one was interested in how much you had or didn't have.' The people here didn't pass judgment on other people's lives, whether they were Moroccan, gay, black, or walking around with two heads! Channelize knew she couldn't bear to spend any more time in Spain. She just wasn't stimulated there any more, especially after experiencing a place with such normality and freedom of choice. It was obvious to Channelize, as she watched the French children playing with other kids of different ethnic backgrounds, that the same values were instilled in them, too.

Darius and Channelize, found a small French bistro, which Darius has spotted a few days before. Next door to the bistro was a quaint little book shop with advertisements in the window. They both stopped, as they often did to peer through the window, Darius was usually looking for a good deal on a car, or computer equipment. As they browsed through the ads in the window, Channelize observed a small card tucked away in a corner.

**Tenants required by private landlord.
2 bed, kitchen, bathroom, City Center Apt,
400 per month. Contact...**

She continued to read every line eagerly.

"Look at this, Darius, it sounds perfect for us," Channelize said, excitedly. "Let's take the number and give them a call. Maybe we can view it while we're here."

Darius agreed, and typed the telephone number into his mobile phone.

"OK," he said. "We will call them when we get back to Simon's. Now, can we get something to eat?" he said impatiently. "My stomach thinks my throats been cut!"

During their lunch, Channelize could hardly contain herself and kept babbling on to Darius about the prospects of the apartment being an ideal place for them.

"Hey, calm down," he said, smiling, but touched by Channelize's enthusiasm. "We haven't even seen it yet. For all you know, it may not be suitable for us," he said.

Channelize tucked into her food. She wasn't the slightest bit interested in negative comments from Darius. She had a gut feeling that fate was playing a hand.

After Penny had heard the news about the apartment, she proceeded to call the telephone number that Darius had installed in his phone. Penny felt it was best if she made the call so that she could translate for Darius in French. However, it soon became clear that owner of the apartment was English. Her name was Sarah. After Penny had asked the appropriate questions, she was informed by Sarah that the only requirements were a monthly deposit, and a signed contract by the tenants, to secure her property. Sarah and Penny concluded the phone call by arranging for Channelize and Darius to view the property the next day. Sarah advised them to collect the keys from her friend, Monsieur Calneau.

That night, Channelize could hardly sleep. She was so looking forward to seeing inside the apartment and desperately hoped it would be suitable for them both. A few of the agency properties they had seen were over-priced and depressingly small. She curled up next to Darius, who was already fast asleep. She hugged him tightly and decided she would try to contain herself until the following morning. Darius was right, it was better for her not to get her hopes up.

It was eleven o clock in the morning. Darius and Channelize had arranged to meet Monsieur Calneau outside a small newsagents, which was situated on one of the many cobbled alleyways, lined with bookshops and coffee shops. The apartment block was facing the newsagents. Monsieur Calneau was waiting outside, and approached them. He was a tall, distinguished, grey-haired man. He had a healthy glow to his face and deep smile lines on the outer corners of his eyes. He sported a neatly trimmed, salt-and-pepper coloured beard. Channelize surmised he was probably in his early fifties. His dark suit was tailored and designer. Underneath his jacket he wore a black, roll-neck sweater, and a Gucci belt around the waistline of his trousers. He extended his hand in a friendly gesture to Darius and Channelize.

"Monsieur Michaels and Madame Develario? he inquired, in a softly spoken, French accent.

"Oui. You must be Monsieur Calneau?" replied Darius, shaking his hand.

"Oui," he confirmed. Then, pointing to the top floor of the apartment block he said, "It ees up there, Monsieur. Apartment number 3t. When you have finished, please return these keys to my wife in the newsagent's." He handed Darius a set of keys.

"The large one ees for the grand door, la petit cle, oh, excuse my English, Monsieur," he said, frustrated with himself. "The small key, ees for the apartment, okay?" He smiled apologetically. "Merci beaucoup!". He looked at his gold watch. "Pardon, now, I ave to go."

"Merci,' replied Darius and Channelize. Monsieur Calneau left.

Channelize could hardly contain herself as Darius opened the large wooden doors to the entrance hall. Directly inside the doorway was a row of mail boxes, Channelize's eyes studied the pebble-dashed walls inside the corridor. She noticed they were in dire need of a paint job and appeared quite old and shabby. The brilliant white walls were now a faded tobacco-yellow, with clusters of dried paint, peeling and chipping over the dismal brown, slated floor tiles. They approached a large and quite impressive spiral staircase but, as they placed their feet on each step, they could feel some of the tiles crunching beneath them. Most of them were broken and unstable and in need of some serious maintenance, thought Channelize. The appearance of the stairway walls seemed to worsen, the more flights they travelled. They were grubby, dirty and stained with hand prints. Channelize walked tentatively up the stairs, her enthusiasm broken and unimpressed. She scrutinised every inch and was disappointed by the tacky, chipboard, mis-matched doors to some of the other apartments.

'Well, at least it's clean. There's no litter or nasty odours… It just needs a bit of a face lift," Darius expressed, after reading the look of disdain on Channelize's face. They continued the flights of stairs until they reached the top. Darius turned the keys and opened the door to the apartment. Channelize was already totally deflated by what she had already witnessed. She couldn't see how the apartment could possibly lift her very sunken spirits. However, they were here now, she thought to herself, miserably. They may as well get it over with.

As they both stepped inside, Channelize could hardly believe the vista in front of her. It was beautiful! She stood in the small hallway, gawping like a child at Disneyland, trying to take it all in. The floor was tiled throughout with brilliant white tiles. She slowly walked from the hallway into the living room space, which opened out like a flower in bloom. The living room was bursting with vibrant-coloured furnishing, and stylish French artwork. Facing Channelize were two of the large, trade-mark French windows, which opened onto a view of the streets. There were two bedrooms, a master bedroom and a smaller, guest bedroom. The bathroom was a suitable, average size, facing a separate fitted kitchen with plenty of storage space. It was exactly the type of place they were looking for, thought Channelize. It had everything they required — even the location was perfect!

Darius had been wandering in and out of the rooms, too. Neither of them had said a word to each other since they had entered the apartment. They had both been overcome with shock. Finally, they stopped and stood together in the living room, when Darius broke the silence.

"Well, what do you think?" he asked.

Channelize took another look around the living room admiringly. "Oh! I love it. It's just… just ideal for us, Darius.

"Oh yeah?" Darius teased. "What about the shabby staircase, and all the steps we have to climb. I thought you didn't like the thought of that?"

"Oh, Darius, don't be silly!" retorted Channelize, already fluffing up the cushions on the sofas and straightening the throws. "That's not a problem, really? After all, we will live inside the apartment, not in the entrance hall! I'm sure we could get used to that and look, Darius, look at the view from this window. We are on top of everything."

Darius walked over to the window and embraced Channelize.

"I take it, we like this one then?" he said, smiling down at her.

"Oh, yes, Darius," she sighed. Channelize looked at Darius coyly. 'I mean, I might just rearrange the furniture a little… and put some lace up at this window…"

The alterations were endless. Darius listened patiently, just nodding his head when it was needed. He listened all the way down the stairs, in and out of the newsagents and all the way back to Simon and Penny's house. Channelize seemed to have a case of verbal diarrhoea! Darius called Sarah and accepted the apartment. They were pleased that things were beginning to fall into place. The ten-day break had certainly been productive. Darius had a good job with Simon, renovating old French houses, which would give him a regular income for a while. They had also found their ideal apartment, within their price range. Channelize went to bed that night feeling exhilarated! A new set of opportunities were finally beginning to unfold for them. A fresh start was just around the corner, thought Channelize. But her thoughts were stifled, when she thought of the mountain of organising that lay ahead, both in France and in Spain. She curled up next to Darius — he was already dead to the world. He hadn't really caught up with his sleep properly after the long journey. Or maybe, thought Channelize, it could be the after effects of the operation. She rolled over to him and gave him a gentle kiss on the cheek. She knew she couldn't fall asleep yet, she had far too much on her mind.

18

The return journey from France was just as long and tiring as it had been, getting there. However, Channelize's thoughts were optimistic and refreshed. She knew that they had discovered something wonderful from their visit to France, which had made them both feel closer and more secure with the outlook of their future together. All of the arrangements had been finalised with the apartment and Darius had managed to pay the first month's rent and the deposit. They had been informed by Sarah, the landlady, that they could have the keys and move in on the first day of December. There was a lot to prepare and saying goodbye to her mother just before Christmas — well, Channelize knew that would be the most heart-wrenching part, and certainly wasn't something she was looking forward to.

It felt very strange to Channelize, waking up in her own bed, the next morning, but she had to admit that it was comforting to feel the sun beaming through the windows and the warmth in the air. She left Darius sleeping and crept out of bed, heading for the kitchen to make some tea. She walked out to the terrace, unlocked the gate and checked the post box. No bills! That was a light relief, she thought. She monotonously muddled through the excessive pile of out-of-date newspapers and pamphlets, until she spotted a white, oblong envelope written in black, ball point pen, with her name on it. She slowly walked to the kitchen curiously staring at the writing, it was not familiar to her at that moment. She placed the letter on the table, made the tea, then sat down and tore open the envelope. It read:

Dear Mum,

How are you? You will be pleased to know that I am out of prison and living with Aimee. I have really missed you and would love to see you soon…

Channelize's eyes widened. It was from Brook! She was so excited and read the letter as fast as she could. It was all good news and Brook sounded happy and relieved to be back to normality. She didn't want to waste another minute and ran to the phone and dialled Aimee's number. Aimee answered.

"Hello, who's calling, please?" she asked, politely.

"Aimee, how are you, my love. It's Aunt Channel. Can I speak to Brook?"

"Hi Auntie, yeah. He is just having something to eat, I will get him for you." Channelize felt as if she could physically combust at the end of the phone. Her stomach was churning with anticipation as she waited impatiently to hear her son's voice. It had only been a few seconds, however, it felt like a lifetime. Her excitement was halted as she heard a pleasant, deep, masculine voice at the other end of the line which, at first, she didn't recognise. She could hardly believe that it was Brook!

"Hello, Mum!" Before he could say another word, Channelize's emotions exploded.

"Oh my God! Brook, it's really you. You sound so different... so grown up. How are you, my darling? I only got your letter today, as you see, we have been away... to France. We are moving there. Oh my goodness, Brook, I'm sorry, I'm just rattling on. I'm just so overwhelmed and excited. It's just so fantastic to hear your voice!"

"All right, Mum, calm down!" he laughed. 'I'm fine, really I am and I'm so sorry..."

Channelize interrupted him quickly, "Don't you dare say that! Like I said in the letter, part of this awful experience was my fault too, for not being there for you."

"Mum, I'm a man now. I knew what I was doing. You always brought me up to know right from wrong, so I knew the difference, Mum. I just got greedy, that's the bottom line," he replied apologetically.

As Channelize listened, the tears started to flow. He was such a special boy... or man now, she thought. He had always been there for her through everything with Paul and also through the death of his sister and had never blamed her for any of her dubious choices.

She felt like she owed him so much and was

desperate to see him.

"Oh no, Mum... you're not crying, are you?" Brook asked, as he heard the faint sniffles at the other end of the telephone.

"No... no," she replied, as she cleared her throat. "I was just thinking how brave you are and how lucky I am to have a son like you, and whatever happens, I will always be so proud of you. I want to come over to see you as soon as possible, would that be all right?" she asked.

"That would be great, Mum, I was hoping you would say that! I will sort it all out with Aimee, but there's plenty of room." His voice sounded so anxious and excited. For one split second, Channelize could hear her little boy in him again.

Channelize briefly spoke to Aimee about the visit. She arranged to book a flight as soon as possible. In the back of her mind, she wanted desperately to see Brook and spend as much time as she could with him, but unfortunately, she had the commitment of packing and sorting the relocation out with Darius. There's no way she could expect Darius to do all the work on his own, so the quicker she booked the flight, the better, she thought. Channelize decided to go to England for one week and explain to Brook her dilemma of not being able to stay longer. However, as soon as she was settled in France, he could come over as often as he liked. She planned to spend as much time with Brook now as possible.

When Darius emerged from the bedroom, Channelize was excited to tell him the news. Even though she felt guilty about leaving him, she was hoping that he would understand.

"Of course you should go," Darius replied. 'I'm sure I can get on with the packing while you're gone. Anyway, it will keep me busy and give me something to focus on."

"Are you sure you don't mind?" replied Channelize. "I really need to see Brook, and I couldn't possibly wait until we were settled in France. This is the best and probably the only time for a few months," she explained. However, Darius didn't seem to have a problem with her plans and at one point even joked that he would finally have some peace!

The flight arrangements were booked for a week later. Channelize and Darius arrived at the airport in Madrid at nine o'clock in the morning. Channelize's flight was due to leave at eleven thirty, so they had plenty of time to check in the suitcase and relax in the airport cafeteria for a coffee and a snack. It felt a little strange to be leaving Darius, as they had spent so much time together lately. However, Channelize knew it would only be seven days and she had left Darius with plenty of work to do. They sat and discussed their plans for France. Channelize gave Darius some ideas with regard to the packing, items which she felt could be packed, and items to be discarded.

"Okay, I think I know what to do. You've told me

a dozen times, plus you have left a list, as long as the great wall of China!" he mocked. "I'm sure I will cope, Channelize," he said, smiling and rolling his eyes. He leaned over the table and kissed her tenderly.

"You just go and have a lovely time and don't forget to tell Brook I said hello. Tell him I am looking forward to meeting him in France soon."

The time had flown by when Channelize heard the announcement over the speaker, that the plane for the East Midlands flight to England, was now boarding.

She hugged and kissed Darius passionately and said goodbye, before making her way through security and to boarding gate number five. It felt strange to Channelize to be completely alone. She had been so used to Darius being right by her side. She quickly turned her thoughts to seeing Brook in England. She hadn't been home in so long. She started to feel pangs of excitement as she boarded the plane and took her seat. She was very lucky and had managed to get a seat nearest to the middle exit doors, which had more than enough leg room. As she took out her magazine and made herself comfortable, a small, frail old lady sat down next to her.

"Hope you don't mind if I sit here?" she said, in a timid voice and projecting a tiny smile on her thin painted lips. Channelize assumed she was in her mid-seventies. She had white curly hair, sunken ice-blue eyes, and a small, pointed nose. Her skin was thin, sallow and wrinkled.

She wore layers of clothing as if she was prepared for the chill in the English air.

"No, of course not," replied Channelize, as she helped the old lady manoeuvre her bag and thick winter coat, underneath the seat.

"Ah, thank you. I think I will probably need that in England," she said gesturing to the coat. "Still, I've had enough of the sun now. I've been out to visit my son for ten days, but oh, that heat can get a bit too much, at my age," she said, with a grimace on her face. "Anyway, my name's Meredith. Thought I should introduce myself as we will be travelling companions for the next couple of hours," she said, extending her frail tiny, hand to Channelize.

"Oh, yes," Channelize replied, shaking Meredith's hand very gently. "My name's Channelize. Strangely enough, I'm going to visit my son, just as you are just leaving yours." Meredith saw the irony, and chuckled with Channelize. Her little joke seemed to break the polite stiffness between the two of them. From that moment on, they were engaged in conversation for the rest of the flight. Meredith spoke about her son and his family. Apparently, he was married to a Spanish lady, and had been living in Spain for twenty years. He was her only child, so she had often travelled to Spain to visit him and her grandchildren. However, she explained, that she found it difficult to cope with the heat, now that she was older. One conversation seemed to lead into another. Channelize enjoyed listening to her. Meredith had such a gentle tone of voice, almost hypnotic, and before they both knew it, the pilot announced they would be touching down at East Midlands airport within the next ten minutes.

It was a safe, smooth descent onto the runway. It wasn't long before the lights were switched on and the passengers were busily pulling their items out of the overhead cupboards. They all seemed very anxious and impatient to get out of the aircraft. Channelize and Meredith sat patiently, watching and waiting for a chance to make their move. As the plane started to empty out, Channelize assisted Meredith with her bags and they both walked to the customs desk together still engrossed in conversation.

'Well, I guess you will soon be seeing your son, once we get through those doors. Are you excited?" asked Meredith, with a twinkle in her eye.

"I feel very excited and very nervous. I want to make every minute count," replied Channelize, as she could see the mass of anxious faces waiting in the arrivals' terminal.

19

Meredith's husband was there to greet her when they passed through the glass doors and into the arrivals' terminal. She introduced him to Channelize, as Jack and explained to him how much she had appreciated Channelize's company and help, on the flight. They said their goodbyes, and Channelize was left standing alone, looking around for Aimee and Brook. Suddenly, she felt someone's hands cover her eyes from behind and then she heard a masculine voice whisper in her ear, "Guess who?" She turned around and looked up. Standing taller than she was, with a dashing smile on his face, stood Brook. Her face lit up with joy as she gave him the biggest hug she could muster from her tiny frame.

"Goodness, Brook, let me look at you!" she said, stepping back from him. "You have grown so tall and so handsome!" she cried. "It's just so good to see you after all this time. And look, a little goatee beard!" she teased, as she tugged at the black stubble growing around his chin. Channelize was pleasantly surprised at how well he looked. His hair was jet-black with shiny, soft, black curls, similar to Fabergé's she thought, as a moment's flashback triggered in her memory. She couldn't believe how much Brook looked like his father now. He was casually dressed in jeans and a thick, navy-blue sweat shirt with New York Yankees emblazoned on the front. He was wearing his favourite footwear — designer trainers.

"Haw are ya, Mum? It's great to see you, too, and you look well. Looks like the Spanish climate has been good to you," he said, still beaming from ear to ear. Brook's smile had always been infectious. He told Channelize that Aimee was waiting in the car park, so they quickly made their way to the car.

Channelize listened attentively, as Brook and Aimee told her their news throughout the drive to Aimee's house. Aimee had taken a new job working in a major high street bank, which she really enjoyed. She had also been making arrangements to marry her long-time boyfriend, Thomas, the following summer. Brook had some news, too, which came as a bit of a shock to Channelize. He had been seriously thinking of moving to America to start a new life and spend time with his father, who lived in New York.

Aimee's house was small, but comfortable, and situated just off a main high street, filled with shops and old-fashioned English pubs. It felt great for Channelize to be home in England, as she hadn't quite realised just how much she had missed all the familiar sights, which she often took for granted when she had lived there. She loved the red double-decker buses, the wide, good-quality roads, the pretty, well-kept English gardens. She almost felt as if she was in a foreign country, everything looked and felt so alien to her.

Channelize spent most of the week cooking the meals that Brook loved and totally spoiling him. They spent days out shopping and taking in the sights.

"Things have certainly changed around here," Channelize commented to Brook, as they sat in a coffee shop in one of the massive shopping centres.

"Do you miss it then, Mum… England, I mean?" asked Brook.

"Yes, I think I do, more than I expected and I really miss you," she answered, feeling her eyes begin to well up with tears.

"Mum, don't start that again. We're meant to be having a happy time together," Brook said, wiping the tears from Channelize's face. She pulled out a tissue and blew her nose. She knew that this week would fly by and it had. She only had three days left, to spend with her son. Channelize looked at Brook and smiled.

"Do you know how good it is to see you, Brook?" she paused and hesitated. "I want to ask you a question, but you don't have to answer, if you don't want to."

Brook looked curious, "Okay. Fire away," he replied.

"What was prison life like for you, son?" asked Channelize, tentatively.

Brook looked down at the table, swirling his spoon around in his coffee cup. It was obvious to Channelize that he felt uncomfortable. He was silent for a few seconds, while Channelize held her gaze. "Just help me understand what you've been through, Brook. What was the worst part?" asked Channelize, gently.

Brook sat back in his chair, folding his arms and tapping one finger on his pursed lips.

"I think the worst part, Mum, is losing your freedom, being locked up from seven o'clock in the evening until eight o'clock in the morning. The food is crap — nothing like yours!" he said managing to break a smile. He continued. "You don't really know what type of people you're remixing with? Even though I was sent to an open prison, which incidentally, had pretty good sports facilities, it was no holiday camp! Luckily, I made goods friends with a few of the wardens there, who gave me light, easy jobs, due to me not using my right hand, too well? He cleared his throat. "But on the whole, it was tolerable, at least for four months, anyway. Most of the people on my wing were theft and fraud cases, so nothing too dangerous. I was only allowed visitors once a week, so it was always great to see Aimee and Thomas. I was really thrilled to receive your letter. It actually kept me going... Oh yeah, I put all the photos on my headboard so they were the first things I saw when I woke up."

They spoke more about Brook's prison life, as they walked home. Channelize was pleased that Brook was prepared to open up to her about his crime and his time served. She felt he had learned a valuable lesson. He had categorically stated that he never wanted to go back to prison again. Channelize could tell that he had grown up. He was level-headed, focused and had an air of maturity about him which she hadn't seen before. Ironically, prison had made a man of him. He was no longer that cute, happy-go-lucky teenager, she had left behind. His personality had developed a more cynical side. Channelize couldn't quite put her finger on it. She sensed it would be a similar feeling to when a woman is raped. However, not in a physical way, but in a mental way. Something about Brook's personality had been raped, and because she was his mother, she had noticed that behind Brook's infectious and dazzling smile, the light was not as bright as it had been before.

It was the last day of Channelize's visit. She had spoken to Darius a few times over the week and it sounded like he had finished most of the packing. He had told Channelize it was mainly her clothes, shoes and other personal items that needed to be packed. He had joked with Channelize that he, in fact, had done the easy part. That evening, Channelize, Brook, Aimee and Thomas went to the Harvester. It was a large, family pub, which laid on a fantastic hot buffet meal consisting of lamb and beef with gravy, various vegetable dishes, roast potatoes and Yorkshire pudding. Channelize was overwhelmed. She hadn't eaten good, old-fashioned English food for a while, and she enjoyed every morsel. They had a wonderful evening, laughing and joking together. Channelize amused them with some of the stories from the ex-pats, and how she had nick-named some of them the 'clucking hens'. Everyone seemed happy and relaxed, apart from Channelize. Her evening was tinged with sadness, as she took her final photos of her last night spent with Brook, Aimee and Thomas.

Looking out of the window as the plane ascended from the runway, Channelize could see in the distance the tiny, red-slated rooftops of the English houses, which by now appeared to be the size of dolls' houses. She said goodbye to the patchwork-quilted landscape as the plane rose higher into the grey, overcast clouds. She sat back into her seat and wondered what her son would be doing at that moment. She gently wiped away the tears from her cheeks. It had been painstakingly sad leaving the family and especially Brook. However, she felt as if she had achieved something in her visit. She had managed to rekindle the fun and trust in her relationship with her son and she also felt at ease with the knowledge that Brook seemed to have grown up. She realised he had changed and was so much more focused.

They had both discussed his plans for going to America to visit his father and after a while she had come around to the idea. He had plans to get his life on track and try to find work in the music business. He had been to college in his teens to learn about producing. He had sounded excited about pursuing that area as a career. His father was quite wealthy and had offered to help with funding. Channelize felt it was the least his father could do, after having an extra-marital affair and abandoning Brook from the age of two, she thought, cynically. Channelize had so much to think about, and eventually dozed off into a deep sleep. She was woken by the gentle touch of a hand from a flight attendant.

"Would you like to fasten your seat belt, madam? We will be landing in approximately ten minutes," she said, giving Channelize a robotic, yet radiant smile. Channelize slowly came around from her sleep and buckled up for landing. She looked out of the window to see a completely different vista. Blue skies, palm trees and below, the vastness of the Mediterranean Sea. As beautiful as it may have appeared, she couldn't help compare it to a child who was receiving a special gift-wrapped present, tied with a magnificent pink bow, only to reveal a large, empty brown cardboard box! It was a strange analysis, Channelize thought to herself? It was the only way she could describe her feelings — her heart was empty, there was no passion. She knew there was nothing here for her in Spain any more, only her mother and Darius.

20

Channelize was overjoyed to see Darius, waiting at the arrivals. They kissed and hugged each other tightly, though she noticed his face looked drawn and tired. She talked rapidly all the way back to the apartment about Brook's plans and the wonders of being back in England. Darius could hardly get a word in edge ways. Finally, after Channelize was drained of conversation, the topic turned to their future plans in France.

"I have spoken to Simon since you have been gone, Channelize, and he says if we have everything wrapped up here, we could stay with him for a week or so, before we move into the apartment in France. He says he could get me started on some work projects, so I could start earning some money for when we move in! What do you think?" asked Darius. Channelize didn't really know what to think. It would mean spending less time with her mother and saying her farewells two weeks earlier than planned. It was all suddenly beginning to sink in. Even though she had tired of Spain, it had been her life for four years. She had genuine friends here and family that she loved. It all seemed too much to think about at that moment. She was full of mixed emotions after leaving Brook and now she would be leaving her mother, too.

'What's wrong?" asked Darius, as they pulled up outside the apartment. 'I thought that's what you wanted, to get out of here as soon as possible?"

"Yeah, it is Darius, but I need to think it through, that's all. Let's talk about it later, okay?" replied Channelize.

'Whatever you want, hun, I thought you would be happy." replied Darius, with a tinge of disappointment in his tone.

Channelize wandered into the apartment, whilst Darius retrieved the suitcase from the boot of the car. She stood in the kitchen and looked around for a moment. Her first instinct, was that it didn't feel like home any more. Darius had obviously been busy and she was pleasantly surprised at the efforts he had made since she had been away. Various-shaped boxes were piled up in the living room. All the pictures and photographs had been packed. Her glass kitchen table had been replaced with the original old-fashioned wooden one that belonged to the owner and as she walked into the living room, she realised that her television stand had been packed and her glass coffee table, both had been replaced by the original old furnishings. It didn't have her stamp on the place any more, she thought. It felt strange and lifeless. Maybe Darius was right. There wasn't really anything to hang on for and money was especially tight, now that she had just been to England.

'What's up, hun?" said Darius, as he caught sight of Channelize standing motionless in the doorway. "Don't worry, we can wait a little longer, if that's what you want. I know you wanted to spend time with Minnie and your friends and say your goodbye properly, so that's fine with me, Channelize. We wait 'til December." he said. He slipped his arms around her waist and embraced her, kissing her passionately. He dropped the suitcase onto the floor and carried Channelize into the bedroom, laying her onto the bed.

"I'm sure there are other immediate matters at hand that will cheer you up," he said, seductively. Darius slowly unbuttoned Channelize's blouse as she lay there, her body quivering with anticipation. They stared alluringly into each other's eyes as her fingers caressed his silky hair. He moaned, as he felt the excitement growing inside his loins. Within moments, they were making love.

Channelize showered and freshened up. She decided it was important to pay a visit to her mother as she knew she would be interested to hear, all about her grandson. Minnie hadn't suspected that Brook had been in prison and thought that the reason Channelize was going to England was to see her son, before moving on to France. She left Darius sleeping. He appeared to be exhausted, in more ways than one. Her mother didn't live far from Channelize and within no time, she was ringing the entrance buzzer.

"Hello," a voice said at the other end.

"Hi, Mum, it's me… Channelize," she replied.

"Oh, you're back then. Come on up," answered Minnie.

Channelize made her way up to the first-floor apartment where Minnie was waiting at the door. She was smiling and looked genuinely happy to see her.

"Ah! It's good to see ya, you're looking well. England must have been good for ya. Come in and I will put the kettle on," she said, drying her hands on her apron and trotting off to the kitchen. Channelize walked straight into the living room to acknowledge Herbert. Her mother's apartment was open-plan, light and spacious with an American-style kitchen so they could natter to each other whilst Minnie made the tea. It was surprisingly modern and homely, considering Minnie's age. She still liked fashionable furnishings and Channelize had encouraged her mother's minimalism in her decoration, introducing her to the 'less is more' theory. However, she noticed she had failed in some areas, as the mantelpiece on the fireplace was cluttered with family photos, and small Irish leprechauns and other memorabilia from Ireland.

Herbert sat in his comfortable, remote-controlled chair in front of the television, where he could raise his legs up and down and assist himself when he needed to sit upright. By the side of his chair was a small tray with mixed chopped fruits and a glass of whiskey. Channelize looked at him, disapprovingly. However, he appeared to look happy enough, she thought. His skin held a healthy glow, which Channelize contemplated might be down to the whiskey. His hair had been neatly cut and his face, recently shaved. He couldn't hold any type of conversation with Channelize. However, he would nod and smile if she asked him a question. Minnie came through with the tea.

"Would ya be wanting to sit on the balcony in the sunshine? That way Herbert can watch the racing in peace," she said, heading outside with the tea. "You will be all right, Herbert. Just outside here if you need me," she said fondly. Herbert nodded, then fixed his eyes on the television. Channelize sat down with her mother and proceeded to tell her the events of the week. She covered everything from Aimee getting married to, the wonderful historic sights in England, that she hadn't appreciated before, and also the decision Brook had made to go to America to pursue a music career and live with his father. Her mother listened and made a few, "Mmm" and "Aha" noises in her throat and nodded in agreement. Finally, she paused.

"How are things with you and Herbert?" asked Channelize. The two years since Herbert had suffered his stroke, seemed to have flown by. Unfortunately, there hadn't been a great deal of improvement.

"Well, it's hard work, Channel, and now I'm that bit older, I am beginning to feel the pressure of it, but at least now we have a better routine and he is standing up on his legs as often as possible, with the Zimmer frame. I mean, what can we do?" she replied, looking

159

downwards and uncomfortably smoothing out her apron.

"I know what you can do, Mum, go back to England," exclaimed Channelize. "There is so much more help for you there, and I made a point of looking into a few options for you on my visit. I've had a word with Tonie, too, she has offered to help and use any influence she has, to get you home."

This time, Minnie didn't dismiss anything Channelize had to tell her. She was stimulated by the options that Channelize had come up with and she looked intrigued.

"Listen, Mum, it looks like I am not going to be around to help you. We are leaving for France at the end of next week," said Channelize, trying to break the news to her mother as gently as possible. Minnie looked flabbergasted.

"But I thought ya would be around 'til the beginning of December. What's the rush?"

Channelize explained to Minnie about Darius's circumstances and the work opportunities for him in France. After a while, Minnie seemed to understand.

"Well, I will miss ya," Minnie said, sadly. "It will be a bit quieter, that's for sure. But I do think Darius is a good man, he has definitely been good for you, Channelize. You've been off the heavy drinking for a while now and you seem a lot happier since you both got together, so I guess, all I can do is wish you both well." She stood up and before collecting up the cups and plates, she leaned down and kissed Channelize gently on the forehead, as a small tear ran down her cheek. She quickly composed herself and said abruptly,

"Ah! Well, I have to get on now. Herbert will be wanting his dinner." She slid through the patio doors and into the kitchen.

21

The next two weeks passed by quickly for Channelize. She had continued to pack all of her clothes and personal items. She was quite overwhelmed with the number of packages she and Darius and managed to collect between them. Darius had been to his house to collect tools and equipment that he would need for France and working with Simon. His work van was completely jammed packed from floor to ceiling, but eventually it was all finished. This weekend would be their last one in Spain, as they had decided to travel on the following Monday. Channelize and Darius had arranged to meet up with a few friends in Angelo's, on the Saturday evening, to say their farewells. Amelia would be there with Yusef, Minnie and a few of her friends from Ireland, Steve and Suzanne, and Lenny had said he wouldn't miss it. It was left very much as an open invitation.

Darius and Channelize turned up at Angelo's at around nine o'clock. The bar was just beginning to fill up with the evening's revellers and the evening's entertainment was a male Spanish singer and a Flamenco dancer. It wasn't long before Minnie joined them with her friends from Dublin. She had made an effort to book a sitter for Herbert tonight, which was unusual for Minnie. She hadn't been out on a night like this, since Herbert had his stroke. Channelize loved her mother's friends, she had always felt close to the Irish people she had befriended in Spain, most of them being from Dublin. They were kind, thoughtful people and would always look in on Minnie and Herbert when they visited Spain. Most of them owned holiday homes there, and were big spenders in the Angelo's bar. Channelize knew that with the crowd of friends her mother brought along, it was sure to be a party night.

Shauna, who was one of Minnie's friends, turned to Channelize and said, "So, you're off to France?"

Channelize nodded. 'Well, don't you worry, Channelize, we will be given ya a right royal send-off, tonight," she said, as she winked suggestively at Darius. "Now, what will ya be havin, and make it a real drink, not that weak tap water you call, wine! Anyhow, ya will be havin' enough of that when you get to France, and don't forget yer froggy legs and yer snails… yuck!" she said, grimacing and laughing raucously.

She nudged Channelize in the arm, and ordered two double brandies for Darius and Channelize. Amelia and Yusef turned up next, followed by Suzanne and Steve. By the time the entertainment started, there was quite a crowd. Channelize wasn't sure if it was the two double brandies kicking in, or the fact that she was surrounded by friends and people that she loved. Either way, she felt on top of the world.

It was turning out to be a fantastic evening. Channelize was constantly on the dance floor showing off her Flamenco dancing skills with her mother and all her Irish friends. Even Amelia and Darius joined in the fun. As the evening drew to a close, Amelia sat down beside Channelize.

"It's been a really happy night tonight. I've enjoyed myself. It's a pity about the circumstances, though," she said, squeezing Channelize's hand. "Indeed, to tell you now, in case I don't get to see you before you go, I will really, really miss you Channelize. You have been such a good friend. And who will these people have to talk about, now that you've gone? They will just have to find another poor victim, I suppose." She giggled.

"I suppose," replied Channelize. 'I certainly won't miss being verbally targeted by those 'clucking hens!'" Channelize turned to Amelia and looked deadly serious.

'I have to ask a favour of you, Amelia," she said, holding both her hands tightly.

"What is it, Channelize? You know I will do whatever I can," replied Amelia, nervously.

"I want you to take care of Minnie, or at least call me if anything happens or if she needs anything. Can you do that for me?" asked Channelize, with sheer desperation written on her face.

"Oh! is that all. Of course I will. I will help her as much as I can. I love Minnie like my own mother, you know that, Channelize. Anyhow, she will be company for me, too, after you go," replied Amelia, relieved that it wasn't anything more sinister. The effects of the alcohol were now beginning to well and truly show in Channelize's slurred speech. She managed to tell Amelia, in the best way she could, how her sister Tonie was trying arrange for supported home assistance in England, for Minnie and Herbert. As she told her story to Amelia, she gazed over at her mother, who was enjoying all the fuss and attention she was receiving. Channelize thought her mother looked radiant and almost looked like her old self. She had visited the hairdresser for the occasion and had applied a minimal amount of make-up. She wore a classic, green chiffon dress which matched the colour of her Irish eyes and a small gold bracelet with matching earrings. The image she portrayed that evening was of health, beauty and happiness, Channelize wanted to capture that image in her head and her heart, forever. She had underlying fears, which she hadn't even told Darius, of never seeing her mother again. Minnie was well into her golden years and with the struggles that she had already gone through, only God knew, how much time she had left.

Suddenly, the music stopped, all of the crowd looked around and saw what was happening. Walking slowly into the main bar from the kitchen was Angelo himself, carrying a huge cake lit up with candles. The music started to play 'When will I see you again' by Diana Ross and the Supremes, as Angelo walked over to the table where Channelize and Amelia were sitting, placing the cake down in front of her. Everyone in the bar crowded around and started to clap as Darius joined Channelize. All Channelize could see were smiling, happy faces.

"We just wanted to give you both a good send-off, Channelize, and wish you well on your journey. You have been a good customer and helped to keep me in business," teased Angelo. The people clapped and heckled her to blow out the candles. With one almighty breath, Channelize and Darius blew them out, the crowd roared and clapped and the Flamenco music started again. The night was one to remember and it was a send-off that Channelize never really expected. She hadn't realised that through everything she had been through here, in this little Spanish town, there were actually genuine people who cared about her. Suddenly, her faith in mankind had been restored. With everything that had been going on, she hadn't realised that standing in a dark corner of the bar, was Yanni. His sad, docile eyes met hers. For a brief second, he mustered up what seemed like a genuine smile and raised his hand to salute Channelize. Luckily, she didn't have time to respond before she was whisked away, by Darius, onto the dancefloor.

Sunday was a quiet, convalescing day. Channelize and Darius were both very hungover from the previous evening and moved through the apartment sluggishly, checking for any important items they may have missed or left behind. Neither of them felt like exerting too much energy. They were leaving at six o'clock in the morning so most of their journey would be in the daylight. It was a day for wrapping up any loose ends and for heartbreakingly fond farewells. Channelize did not linger too long after kissing Herbert and her mother goodbye. She had said all that she needed to say to Minnie the night before, which had been very emotional for the two of them. Amelia had given her a small square jewellery box and a sealed card, with strict instructions not to open until she was on the move to France. She had packed the items safely in her handbag. Darius and Channelize decided to get some sleep, before their long journey and set the alarm for four o'clock in the morning. She had prepared baguettes, fruit and soft drinks for their journey, and before long, they were winding down the deserted roads at dawn. Away from Spain, heading for France and their new life.

22

Two weeks had passed, since their arrival in France. Channelize and Penny had got to know each other quite well in that time. They had shared stories about their families and Penny had given Channelize snippets of useful information about living in France and the French customs. Penny had been living in the country for several years and was already fluent in the French language. Channelize spent much of her time, while Darius and Simon were at work, reading French books, that Penny had given her, studiously trying to learn the language. It was strange and awkward for Channelize at first, living in someone else's house, especially people that she didn't really know that well. She would often find herself staring out of the window onto the wintry garden. The trees were naked and eerie, twisted in strange talon-like, shapes. The leaves were brown and lifeless, scattered like a carpet over the lawn and patio. The beautiful garden now had a cold and ghostly feeling. Channelize's heart felt heavy, pangs of extreme loneliness would engulf her as she stood there, motionless, daydreaming and wondering what Minnie and Amelia were doing at that moment. She held the little pink gift box in her hand and gently touched the heart-shaped necklace, which Amelia had brought her with 'Friends Forever' engraved on the back. She missed them both so much, much more than she ever would have imagined. She really missed the giggles and the childlike banter of their 'ladies-that-lunch days'.

Penny was a completely different person to Amelia. She was around the same age, yet she seemed serious and detached. Although, she was an accommodating and pleasant person, her life was mostly wrapped up in her home and her children. She lacked that fun and warmth that Amelia had, thought Channelize. Some days she would only pass Penny on the stairs, as she rushed to and fro with appointments and school runs. The house was cold and unfamiliar too. It was always so quiet, you could hear a pin drop. There was seldom a radio or television playing, which Channelize couldn't understand or get used to. Obviously, that's how Penny and Simon preferred to live their life, she thought. She was in no position to complain, as she and Darius were more than grateful for their help, but the silence only added to her feelings of isolation. She always looked forward to seeing Darius when he arrived home in the evening. He would hold her and comfort her as they lay in bed together, reassuring her that their situation wouldn't be for long, always trying his hardest to lift her spirits. He would speak positively about their new apartment, counting down the days until they had their own space and familiarity.

Channelize was quietly relieved when the first of

December arrived. Simon had given them a hand with the boxes. It was the first time he had been inside the apartment. He was surprisingly, impressed.

"It's really nice and a good size," he said, as he placed one of the heavy boxes down in the living room, the sweat pouring off his brow.

"Would you like a drink? Tea or something, Simon?" asked Channelize.

He smiled wryly. "Yeah, I could do with a cuppa, I thought you would never ask," he said.

Channelize walked into her new kitchen and looked around, inside, she was elated. There were still unopened boxes piled up and Channelize couldn't wait to start displaying all her family photos and trinkets. Darius appeared at the kitchen doorway.

"Guess you want tea, hun?" she said, playing mother in her very own kitchen and setting up the cups, milk and sugar. He placed his arms around her waist.

"Happy?" he said, giving her a tight squeeze. She turned to face him, placing her arms around his neck.

"Yes, and you?" she replied, pecking him on the lips.

"Of course, if you are," he replied, returning her affection. He turned to look at the boxes.

"Well, you have plenty to keep you busy! Next week, when I get paid, we can go shopping and buy some bits and pieces for the place. I have something else to ask you, too," He said mysteriously. Channelize rolled her eyes flirtatiously.

"Oh no, not while Simon is in the living room," she giggled,

"Not that!" replied Darius, snuggling into her neck. "How would you feel if Judith, my mother, came for Christmas?"

It was a mad rush for Channelize to get everything organised for the Christmas holidays. She had been so busy with the apartment. Firstly, she started with the bathroom, detaching the fungicidal shower curtain that hung there. 'Yuck!" she said, looking at it with contempt and throwing it to one side. She replaced it with a brand new, aqua and lemon lace design. She brought aqua and lemon furry bath mats and matching towels. She delicately hung her crocheted hanging basket in a corner, displaying it with a thick green, fern plant. Next, she moved onto the living room, folding away the throws and exposing two beautiful lilac sofas. She brought matching cushions and white roller blinds for the living room windows. She enjoyed the beauty of the French windows when the blinds were rolled up in the daytime. Then, she moved into the guest bedroom where Judith would be sleeping. She brought a pink and lilac duvet cover, a pair of fluffy lilac throw mats and redesigned the furniture so it appeared warm and compact. She cleaned all the glass on the mirrors and windows, washed all the floors, and last of all set up the small artificial Christmas tree, which she had brought with her from Spain. Judith was arriving on the twenty-second of December, which was in two days' time.

Channelize was happy and satisfied with the work that she had put in and stood back to admire the apartment. Everywhere looked neat and organised, the way she liked it. The floors and windows were gleaming, and the white lights twinkled like stars on the little Christmas tree. The only job left to do, thought Channelize, was the Christmas food shopping. She had already brought her gifts for Darius and Judith and she had sent money in a card to her mother, Amelia and Brook. It was a good feeling for Channelize to actually have some money. It had been a long time since she could treat herself, or other people. Darius had been working non-stop with Simon.

When Darius arrived home from work at six o'clock that evening, he was amazed at all the effort Channelize had gone to, to make the place look homely and seasonal. The tree looked especially magical as it twinkled away in the window. The lights changed sequence on a timer, every few minutes. The gifts had been wrapped with silver paper and red ribbon and placed neatly around the bottom of the tree. Channelize served their evening meal as Darius showered and changed. He joined Channelize in the kitchen.

"Mmm, something smells good. I'm starving," he said as he pulled out a chair and sat down at the table. "Looks like we have both had a busy day!" he said, eagerly tucking into the meal Channelize had placed in front of him.

They spent a lot of quality time together in the

evening as they didn't have television. Most evenings, they would go into the Plaza and sit outside a bar called 'Pierre's' which they had adopted as their own. They enjoyed drinking vin chaud, which was a hot mulberry-red wine, with cinnamon. On these cold, wintry, evenings it certainly took the chill out of the bones. Channelize would order two or three, cupping them in her hand, blowing frantically and sensing the steam rise up into her icy nostrils. The Plaza was buzzing with life this time of year. In the centre and surrounded by the quaint French coffee shops, a giant ice-skating rink had been erected with huge disco lights firmly attached to the surrounding trees, which changed from blue, purple, amber, and yellow, as the music from the large speakers blared out. A mixture of age groups would skate around to the music, wrapped in warm clothing, woollen hats, gloves and scarfs. Channelize loved to sit with Darius holding her piping hot, vin chaud, absorbing the seasonal ambiance and watching the happy smiling faces of the children. The French people oozed a sense of class, romance, tradition and humour. She watched the young males, about Brook's age, romantically linked with their girlfriends, skating around and around on the ice, staring lovingly into their partners' eyes. She was amused by the boisterous fathers clowning around with their children on the ice and listened to the fits of laughter from the children, as their parents would end up with their bottoms on the ice and legs up in the air. Surrounding the ice rink were Scandinavian-style, log

173

cabins, selling various Christmas memorabilia. Channelize's favourite log cabin, sold the traditional, and famous, French crepes. The intoxicating smell of crepes sizzling on the hot plate and the mixed aroma of thick brown chocolate melting in a huge pan, would make Channelize's mouth water.

They had only been living here for a few weeks, however, Channelize and Darius were falling in love with France and the people. There was so much more to do here. Toboggan runs for the kids covered with fake snow, funfairs set up all around the town with various rides, huge ferris wheels, toffee apple stalls, bands and concerts in the parks. The Christmas lights were something Channelize had never seen before in her life. The whole city was full of creativity and artistic flair. There were areas in the city designed to imitate the North Pole, with giant snowmen, polar bears and reindeer. There was an abundance of decorated Christmas trees, lining every street. Channelize was flabbergasted! She noticed the French County Council did nothing to cut corners. She thought to herself, there was no comparison to Spain, where nothing as impressive as this would be laid on. She had mentioned to Darius that she felt the taxpayers' money was well spent. The visual displays were breathtaking and must have been very expensive, she thought.

Both Channelize and Darius' minds were free and stimulated again. There were still moments when Channelize would miss her mother and Amelia, especially at this time of the year, but it had been a surreal experience moving to France. She felt much healthier, even in the few weeks she had been there. She wasn't drinking half as much and was happy to be occupied with other more, enjoyable and interesting things to do.

23

Channelize was nervous and on edge as she waited for Darius to return from the airport with Judith. She had never met his mother and was slightly perturbed that he had invited her for Christmas. They had barely moved into the apartment and there had been so much to prepare. On the other hand, she was grateful to have some female company for a change. She had hardly seen Penny since the day they moved in. The days were long and lonely without Darius or anyone to speak to. She had basically completed all of the unpacking. Now, everything was in its place. Most of the day she spent cleaning or reading her French language books. She had recently enrolled in a French class for two hours a week. It was held in the school around the corner, which was a five minute walk for Channelize. The class had been a god-send, in more ways than one. Channelize had met other English people who had recently moved to France. However, they lived in the surrounding villages. The French teacher's name was Nadia. She was young and attractive, with long, dark, silky hair. Nadia was welcoming and a very conscientious tutor. Her grasp of the English language was flawless. The class was closed now for two weeks during the Christmas holidays, so for Channelize it would be nice to have Judith around to talk to. There was only so much Darius was prepared to talk about with regard to cosmetics, shoes, home furnishings, and cooking!

Channelize checked the apartment for the tenth time. She flushed the toilet again, even though no one had used it. She straightened the towels in the bathroom again) even though no one has used those either. She stood at the doorway of Judith's bedroom, opening and closing the door to see which way would create the desired effect. She decided to leave it closed. She couldn't sit down on the sofa for fear of squashing the nicely puffed cushions. They were so perfectly placed, thought Channelize, and she didn't want to ruin them. She sat down at the kitchen table, placing her elbows on the table and nestling her chin into her cupped hands. She was bored and anxious. She lightly tapped her cheeks with her fingers. All she could do was wait until Darius returned. She thought about lighting a cigarette, but she didn't want the smell to linger in the apartment. She considered smoking it out of the window, but she was worried the fumes may waft inside. Darius and Channelize had agreed not to smoke inside the apartment whilst Judith was visiting. Apparently, Judith suffered with chest problems. Channelize was restless. Her eyes glimpsed the clock, Darius had been about two hours, she thought. Channelize worked out in her head that it would have taken Darius forty minutes to reach the airport. Time would be spent waiting for Judith to come through baggage and arrivals and then motorway traffic.

"J... she should be arriving very soon," she mumbled out loud to herself. She continued impatiently tapping her cheeks.

Twenty minutes must have elapsed, as Channelize sat there, tapping and daydreaming. Suddenly, she heard voices and footsteps climbing up the entrance stairs. Channelize jumped up from the table and quickly straightened the table cloth. She scurried into the bathroom to check her appearance. The voices were outside the door now and Channelize heard Darius turn the key. She stood, nervously waiting, on the other side of the door, presenting herself as if she was about to greet the queen!

"Hi, hun," Darius said, as he entered. He learned towards her and kissed her on the lips. He shuffled the suitcase through the door and placed it down in the hallway. Judith followed behind him. Channelize's first impression of Judith, was that she had a kind, matronly face. She was pale skinned, due to the English weather no doubt, thought Channelize. Her cheeks were flushed pink and her skin remarkably smooth of wrinkles for a woman in her mid-seventies. Her hair was fair, cut to her ears. Channelize thought that Judith resembled an older version of Viv, as her hair was worn in a similar style. She wore a salmon-coloured cashmere jacket, black slacks with a black, woollen sweater underneath. Her make-up was minimalistic.

Channelize greeted her with a friendly smile and kissed her on the cheek.

"Hello, nice to meet you, Channelize," Judith said politely, and then speedily headed for the living room sofa. Letting out a loud sigh of relief, she sat down on Channelize's plumped cushions.

"That's better," she said, slowly removing her coat, gloves and the small scarf from around her neck. Looking up at Channelize, she said wearily, "How on earth do you manage all of those stairs. There are so many of them and some are loose, you know. I didn't think I would ever get to the top alive!" she said, releasing a little chuckle. Channelize noticed straight away that Darius looked like his mother. He had inherited her smile. Simon, however, looked completely different and Channelize couldn't see any resemblance at all. Judith spoke with a slight London accent but it wasn't as broad as Viv's. Her voice was soft and soothing, similar to Meredith's, the old lady she had met on the plane. Channelize was pleasantly surprised at some of Judith's characteristics and she felt nostalgic as she thought of her old friend, Vivien. She was articulate, stimulating and easy going, yet Channelize suspected, hat underneath her conservative and respectable appearance, lay a playful, and comical sense of humour. Channelize felt from that moment, that she would get along with Judith like a house on fire.

It was the morning of Christmas day. Channelize got out of bed early to prepare the turkey and

179

vegetables. Judith was already up, sitting on the sofa, sipping her coffee and attempting to complete a crossword from her English newspaper.

"Good morning, Channelize. Merry Christmas!" she said, jovially.

"Merry Christmas to you, too," replied Channelize.

"I've been up for a while. I find it very hard to sleep in a strange bed," she said, looking over her spectacles at Channelize. 'I'm sure I will get used to it." She lowered her eyes and studied the crossword. "I like doing the crossword, it keeps my mind active. And at my age it wouldn't do to vegetate, would it?" Judith questioned, with a humorous grin on her face.

Channelize smiled back,

"Yes. I know what you mean. I think my mind will vegetate soon if I don't find a job or something to occupy my days. I often do crosswords, too," replied Channelize. She turned and headed for the kitchen. She called over her shoulder,

'Would you like another coffee, Judith? I am just making one."

"Yes, please. Do you need a hand with Christmas lunch?" shouted Judith.

"No, thanks. I think I have it all under control. You relax and do your crossword," Channelize replied.

A few minutes later, Channelize came through to the living room carrying a tray with coffee and biscuits. Judith put down her paper and took her coffee.

"Thank you," she said politely, cooling it with her

lips, before sipping.

"Do you get bored here, Channelize... in the daytime, I mean, when Darius is at work?" she asked.

"Yeah, a bit," replied Channelize. "I do have my French course, but I miss getting together with my mother, or my best friend, Amelia, for a chat. I don't really know anyone here, yet." Judith picked up on Channelize's solemn tone.

"What about Penny, do you see much of her?"

Channelize shook her head. "No. Not really. She seems to be very tied up with the children, and her own business, and that's fine with me," replied Channelize, unconvincingly. Judith looked into her eyes.

"I'm sure we will meet other people soon. We haven't been here that long," Channelize continued, forcing a smile.

"Oh, I'm sure you will," replied Judith, sympathetically.

At that point Darius sluggishly walked out of the bedroom. He rubbed his eyes like a sleepy infant.

"Merry Christmas!" shouted Judith and Channelize in unison. Darius looked startled. They both looked at each other and laughed. "That soon woke you up, didn't it, sleepy head?" Judith teased.

A good time was had by all, as Christmas came and went. Judith appeared to be seduced by France, in the same way Darius and Channelize had been. She had enjoyed all the activities at the central plaza and took a particular liking to the hot mulled wine. She raved about the amazing French food and the people. Simon and Penny had been over to visit Judith once, at the apartment. Judith had confided in Channelize one day and told her that she had never been very close to her son, Simon. He had always been, as she put it, a bit of a 'restless soul'. She hadn't seen much of him since he moved to France. However, Penny and Simon had prepared a lavish meal on the eve of Judith's departure. The next day, Judith said her goodbye's and went back to England. The holidays were over and a new year had begun. The apartment felt empty to Channelize. Darius had gone back to work and she was alone again. Somehow, the loneliness of the apartment had intensified since Judith had gone. She had certainly been entertaining and good company. She had helped to ease the pain, which Channelize may have felt throughout the Christmas period, being away from her mother and Amelia.

The weeks and months flew by. Channelize continued studiously with her language class. She felt quite impressed with herself, as she was able to converse, somewhat, with the natives. She felt confident about going out in the city alone. She would take a book or magazine and sit in a coffee shop, reading and whiling away the hours, as the French people did. The weather was improving. The winter months had passed and spring was in the air. The buds were beginning to shoot from the trees. The migrating birds had returned, chirping merrily on the rooftops. A canvas of yellow tulips and pungent spring flowers, filled the rolling fields of the French countryside. Channelize felt content, however, her heart was heavy. She couldn't understand this dislodged feeling that she had. She felt alien and isolated. As she sat drinking her coffee, she desperately wanted someone to talk to her. She watched the waiter rushing in and out with his tray perched high on his hand, busily taking orders. A man and a woman, possibly husband and wife, she thought, sat at a table holding hands, smiling into each other with amour in their eyes. On another table, Channelize watched, as four women, about her age, were excitedly showing off some items, they had brought from an expensive boutique. They looked independent, well dressed and elegantly groomed. Channelize imagined they all worked for the same large company — best friends, probably, she thought enviously. She watched a small boy and his mother sitting at another table close by. He looked about six years old, to Channelize. He was mischievously blowing bubbles and making gurgling noises into his soda, with a straw. His mother chastised him, before going inside to pay the bill. He raised his eyes above his glass and peered at Channelize. His eyes were beautiful, sapphire blue, and glistened like marbles. He smiled curtly, before lowering his eyes and continuing to play his gurgled symphony inside the glass. Channelize smiled to herself, he reminded her so much of Brook, when he was young and infantile.

Channelize paid the waiter for her coffee and

walked along the busy streets to the apartment. She was in a melancholy mood. She had tried to share her feelings with Darius recently, but he had been rather detached. She often got the feeling that he wasn't even listening to her. She knew he had pressure from Simon with the renovations work they were doing. Simon had told him that the structures of the building in France, were completely different to the way they were built in Spain. They had come to loggerheads a few times over each other's expertise. Channelize was still immersed in her thoughts, as she reached the main door of the apartment block. She was about to put the key in the main door when she was suddenly aware of a crying, whimpering sound coming from the bookshop doorway. As she stopped and poked her head around the pillar, separating the two buildings, she was amazed to see a tiny little dog shivering and scared. It wasn't wearing a collar, its ribs protruded and its eyes bulged with fear. She knelt down and slowly, extended her hand out in friendship. The little dog trembled, and quickly scuttled himself closer into the corner of the doorway.

"Hello, what's your name?" Channelize asked. "It's okay, don't be afraid," she said quietly, gently stroking the dog's ear with her forefinger. She remembered she had a ginger biscuit in her handbag from the coffee shop. She broke a tiny piece off the biscuit and gestured to the little dog. It reluctantly started to smell the biscuit, keeping its eyes firmly fixed on Channelize for any sudden moves. The dog started to lick gently with its little pink tongue and seemed to be enjoying the ginger taste. She placed the morsel on the floor and the little dog demolished it quickly. Channelize gave the dog the rest of the biscuit. It had started to trust her, and manoeuvred slowly towards her. It allowed her to pick it up. It was still shaking with fear, however, Channelize stroked it comfortingly. It licked her cheek and she noticed it had the most beautiful, round, black eyes, extra-long lashes and a cute, black, button nose. It was a charcoal grey colour all over, apart from a paw-sized, white marking on its chest. Its tail was fluffy, and stood upwards as it started to wag, it resembled a woman's powder puff, thought Channelize.

Channelize looked around the street. What could she do with him? she thought, anxiously.

She had realised he was a male, during her examination!

"He must belong to someone?" she said to herself, out loud. She continued to look around, but could see no sign of any frantic person searching for their pet. If she left him in the doorway, she knew there was a possibility of him getting killed on the busy street. The book shop never opened on a Monday either, so no one would be coming in today to find him. The little dog was excited in her arms, he licked and nestled himself into her chest. She couldn't be so cruel as to just leave him there.

"Poor little thing," she said to him. He looked up at her with his sad, puppy-dog eyes. It was quite common in Spain for certain, heartless individuals to abandon their dogs, maybe they had the same problem here, in France, pondered Channelize.

It was late in the afternoon and Darius would be home soon for tea. She must decide what to do.

Channelize stood there for a few seconds, checking up and down the street. No one seemed to be interested in her. People were just busying about with their own lives.

"It's not like I'm stealing you," Channelize said, looking down at the little dog. "But I can't leave you here to face the night, you could be killed! So really, I am just looking after you for a while, until we find your owner. That's not criminal, is it? she asked the dog.

He licked her face happily and wagged his tail. She smiled at him, affectionately, giving him a gentle little hug.

"Okay. Let's go upstairs and I will find you some proper food. Maybe there's some meat left over from last night." She cradled the little dog in her arms, talking to him maternally as she climbed the flights of stairs. Once inside the apartment, she set down a bowl of cold water, and watched him eagerly lap it up.

"You were very thirsty, little pooch," she said, stroking his fluffy little head. "That's it!" cried Channelize. "That's what I will call you... for now, anyway... Pooch!" Pooch looked up at Channelize, the sadness and fear, now gone from his eyes. He wagged his little powder-puff tail, approvingly.

24

Darius was indifferent with regard to Pooch, the little orphaned dog. However, he knew that Channelize had been depressed lately and felt that the little dog may be good for her morale. He spoke to Penny about advertising Pooch in the lost dog section of the local paper, which she had agreed to do. She also said she would put a notice up in the children's school, to see if there was any response. Six weeks passed, and no one had come forward to claim Pooch. Channelize was secretly pleased. She had grown very fond of little Pooch by this time. He would follow her everywhere. Wherever she was, Pooch would be sitting or curled up close by. She would talk to him affectionately, as she ironed and cleaned. He would sit on her lap in the coffee shop, sticking his little nose into her French book or magazine. He was such an inquisitive and funny little dog and Channelize, loved him dearly. She was so excited on the day she could finally take him to the veterinary surgeon to get him vaccinated, and microchipped. This procedure, computerised his name, address, and registered Channelize as his owner. Channelize would have been devastated to lose him and he never let Channelize out of his sight. She came to the conclusion, that he must have been deliberately dumped, and must have found his way to the bookshop doorway. Maybe it was serendipity, that she had found him, and he had found her. Pooch had such a loyal and dependent personality, she didn't think he would have just run away. She wasn't certain in her mind of what the circumstances may have been. All she was sure of, was now Pooch officially, and legally, belonged to her.

Darius and Channelize spent most of their weekends exploring the beautiful countryside of France. They would go for long drives through the long, winding roads of the mountains, going higher and higher as they drove. The views were stunning. Exquisite and very grand French chateaux were vaguely hidden, behind thick dense forest. Around every bend, the endless Rocky Mountains emerged, rising up like gigantic monsters of nature. They were intimidating, yet strangely protective at the same time, thought Channelize. It was as if they were nurturing and guiding you through the snake path. Channelize felt as if she was a small speck of dust, compared to their dominance and enormity. They drove through many, pretty French villages and were in awe of the original, quaint French houses and the acres of neatly tended rows of vineyards. Channelize thought the climate here in France, was perfect for producing the best wines in the world. There was a sufficient amount of rain and an equal amount of sunshine, which seemed to be a perfect combination. Channelize had tasted the wine in France and it was outstanding and of superb quality. She did not profess to being an expert in the wine-tasting field. However, she had indulged in enough of the stuff in Spain, to know a good wine when she tasted it. It was potent. She could definitely not consume the amount she used to in Spain.

She stared out of the window, taking in the beauty of the land, as Darius drove along in his own little world, whistling. She smiled as she thought about how happy she was living here. France had certainly not disappointed her. Their past six months had been surreal. She had been relieved of the worry of her mother, as her sister, Tonie, had managed to secure Minnie and Herbert a residential home for the elderly, and they had both returned to England, shortly after Christmas. It was a one-bedroom apartment, equipped with support railing, hoists, and an emergency cord to call for help. It was perfect! Her mother was now able to take a well-earned rest. She had all the support and care that they both needed. Channelize would speak to her mother constantly, and hoped that herself and Darius could spend Christmas with them, in England, next year. She had invited Minnie over to France for a visit. However, Minnie was too tired now, and feeling her age. She didn't want to travel any more and was more than happy to stay with Herbert in their brand-new, modern apartment.

"Do you fancy stopping off for a drink in this little village, Channelize? I feel I need to stretch my legs, hun," Darius said, arms outstretched and arching his back. Channelize emerged from her thoughts. "You've been quiet. Deep in thought?" he asked.

"Yeah. I was just thinking how much my life… our life, has changed since we have been living here, and how beautiful it is," Channelize said, dreamily.

'I'm glad you're happy, hun. But do you know what will make me really happy?" he said smiling. "Nice, ice-cold beer!"

They parked under a shady tree and walked back along the quiet village street to a bar they had passed. They sat down at a wooden table, underneath a parasol, outside on a small terrace. Pretty pink and white flowers, neatly displayed in hanging baskets, hung on the railings around the main perimeter of the terrace and above the main entrance doors. The bar was situated on a bridge, overlooking a babbling brook, which was overcast with disjointed trees. Channelize appreciated how peaceful and relaxing it was, listening to the sound of the water gently trickling over the stones and the song of the birds, chirping in the trees. The bar wasn't busy, but there were a few people scattered on individual tables.

Channelize noticed a man and woman sitting at a table nearby. He had broad shoulders, brown, short hair, and a prominent nose. He wore a bottle-green short-sleeved shirt, sandals and knee length shorts. She had a round, jovial face, gentle features and a mischievous smile. She had dark-brown, feathered hair, cut to her shoulders, and wore an animal print, short-sleeved top, and white jeans. Channelize glimpsed at the couple, as she overheard their accent, which she couldn't quite place. It didn't sound French, thought Channelize. The barman took their order and within a few minutes, Darius was guzzling down his refreshingly cold beer.

"Just what the doctor ordered," he said, admiring the beer in its frosted glass.

Channelize laughed as she spotted the creamy froth stuck to his lips.

"Good God!" she said, alarmed. "You look as if you have rabies. Maybe I should get you vaccinated next?" They both giggled, as Darius dragged his arm across his mouth.

"That better?' he said.

"Perfect," replied Channelize, and leaned over to kiss the last little creamy bubble from his nose. They talked and playfully joked around for a few minutes, not noticing the man in the green shirt standing behind them.

"Excuse me. Is that your van parked over there?" the man asked. Channelize realised straight away that he had a strong, Scottish accent.

Darius turned around in his seat and replied curiously, "Why, yes. Is there a problem?"

"No, no. Not at all laddie. I was just wondering if you do removals? Me and the wife, have just moved here, about two months ago, and we have bought a house. However, we are having a lot of work done on it at the moment, and need a pile of rubble shifting. Would ya be interested? I would pay ya well." The man smiled at Channelize and introduced himself. "Me name's Jake. And, that's the wife over there… Priscilla." He gestured to his wife and she gave a little wave, smiling broadly. Jake proceeded to tell Channelize and Darius of his plans to renovate an old French house and turn it into three apartments. He had some knowledge of building, but would be looking for extra help in the future.

"Aye! It's a big job," he said wiping the sweat from his brow. His beer had been sitting on his table while he had spoken to them. It would no doubt have been warm by now, thought Channelize.

"Er, why don't you and your wife join us?" said Channelize, hesitantly. Darius agreed. He ordered a beer and a wine for Jake and Priscilla, and two coffees for himself and Channelize. The four of them conversed for a couple more hours that afternoon. It turned out that Priscilla and Jake were in their forties, the same age group as Darius and Channelize. They appeared to have the same interests and the same passion for France and the people. They had visited the Languedoc region many times on holiday, however, they had recently decided to move to France permanently. They were both such great company and Channelize hadn't felt like she had laughed so much in ages. Both Jake and Priscilla were humorous and comical people. They told Channelize and Darius some very unusual and quirky stories. The house they were working on was just around the corner from where Channelize and Darius lived, near to the Central Plaza. Darius arranged to meet up with Jake the next day to take a look at the site.

Darius and Channelize met up with Jake and Priscilla many times after that. They often went out once or twice a week for evening meals or just for drinks. Channelize would invite them to the apartment for dinner and Priscilla would do the same. At last, thought Channelize, they finally had a social life, and some true friends. Darius worked some weekends for Jake, and worked on the week days for Simon. He was constantly busy.

However, their finances were rapidly improving and one day Darius came home with a large box.

'What's that?" asked Channelize curiously, as he placed the box on the kitchen table. She was as impetuous as a child and couldn't wait for Darius to open it. As he pulled the box from the polythene bag, Channelize realised, it was a laptop computer. Channelize looked puzzled. She wasn't the most technical person in the world and hadn't used a computer since she had worked in an office in England, years ago. "It's a computer," confirmed Darius, satisfactorily.

"I can see that! But how do we use it. It looks complicated," replied Channelize. Staring at the picture on the box, as if the lap top was some kind of alien.

"All the instructions are inside. I will set it up after

tea. It will be great for you, Channelize. You always said you wanted to write a book or something. Also, you can keep in touch with Brook, via emails. It even has a web-cam, so you can video-phone him in America!

Channelize looked even more puzzled. She stared at Darius and said, "What's a web-cam?"

Darius looked and her and rolled his eyes. "Oh, dear! Looks like this is going to be harder for me, than I thought," he teased.

Later on that evening, Darius disappeared into the living room to set up the computer. He was immersed in leads and gadgets that Channelize had never seen before. She decided to leave him to it and sat in the kitchen, slowly sipping on a glass of wine. She turned on the radio and started to lose herself in the soothing tones of a French singer. As she sat there she started to daydream about Brook. He had gone to America, to live with his father, shortly after they had arrived in France. He had enrolled on a music production course in an exclusive American College, in New York. Channelize had gathered from his phone calls, that he sounded happy and content with his new life. He had met a girl, her name was Georgia. She was on the same course as Brook, and apparently, he said they had the same interests and lots in common. She was stimulating, intelligent and very creative, according to Brook, and also, very beautiful. He called his mother as often as he could however, it was expensive. He would obviously have to stay in America until his course was finished in three years' time. However, he had promised that he would visit Channelize with his new girlfriend, the following spring break.

Channelize sat, sipping her wine, and remembered her feelings of envy because his father would be spending so much time with Brook, and her feelings of abandonment because, once again, she was separated from her only son. She knew that it was selfish for her to feel like that, but at last she understood how abandoned Brook must have felt when she left him behind in England with no one to turn to. It had not been quite so bad for her, she thought. At least she had Darius. It was no wonder that Brook had got himself into the situation he did, thought Channelize. She had shut him out at that time in her life and detached herself from any form of reality or human contact. He was only eighteen! how could he really cope with all of that. He was still only a child, really, thought Channelize sadly, as she sipped on her wine.

"Mustn't live in the past, Channelize," she said to herself, quietly. "It's time to move forward and try to be happy, the best way we can. And Brook is happy... by the sounds of it." Pooch sat at the foot of the chair looking sympathetically at her, with his adorable, dark eyes.

"Who are you talking to?" asked Darius curiously, as he approached the kitchen door.

Channelize turned red and looked slightly embarrassed. "Oh, just Pooch, and thinking out loud, I guess?" she replied, sheepishly.

'Well, it's all done… Voila!" he said triumphantly. "Let's go and play with our new toy, and I will show you how it works."

25

It was a week before Channelize's forty-fifth birthday. She wasn't looking forward to it — what women did at her age? Another year older and another milestone in her life. It was normal for her to feel depressed, she always did when her birthday was looming over her head, like a persistent vulture! It was a cool, bright summer morning, so Channelize decided to take Pooch for his daily walk before the temperature rose, as it used to in the afternoon. Darius was at work, as usual, so she would need to amuse herself. Pooch was such good company for Channelize and she couldn't imagine her life without him. He always sensed when he was going out for a walk and would spring around happily as Channelize attached his harness and lead. It was Monday, and most of the shops didn't open until later in the afternoon and some didn't open at all. She passed by the newsagents and the bakery shop on the corner, which were always open. It seemed to be an old tradition for the French people to consume large quantities of baguettes. Channelize remembered hearing somewhere, that many of the French people had survived on mostly bread during the Second World War, because it was cheap and would sustain them.

However, Channelize noticed the French people had much more of an expensive palette these days, and would often accompany their simple baguette, with fine quality cheeses, and an ample glass of locally produced, red wine. The Central Plaza was quiet at this time of morning. All the students would have their heads buried in their books at the 'Lycée' or college and the restaurants would be busily preparing the lunch menu for the day, ready for the twelve o'clock stampede. There were a few people reading their newspapers and drinking coffee, sitting outside the Plaza coffee shops. She passed people walking their dogs as she walked with Pooch. They would nod their heads in a friendly gesture and say, 'Bonjour!' toher.

"Bonjour," Channelize would reply, politely.

Pooch and Channelize walked around for twenty minutes or so, taking in the smells of the city and the beautiful architectural sights of the huge, classic French buildings. Channelize felt she could never get bored, looking around at the art and vibrant culture of this wonderful city. Sometimes she had to pinch herself, when in dawned on her that she actually lived in such a beautiful place. Pooch and Channelize decided to sit down on a park bench to rest. Pooch only had short little legs and would get tired easily. Channelize could tell he was ready for their normal park bench resting ritual, as he had already halted by a seat and laid stretched out, underneath.

"Okay," said Channelize, smiling at the little dog.

"I guess it's break time?" She sat down on the bench watching people jogging and cycling past her. Suddenly, her mobile phone started ringing, she popped her hand in her pocket and answered.

"Hello?"

It was Amelia, and she sounded excited.

"Hi, Channelize, have you got time for a quick chat? I have something to tell you."

Channelize relaxed casually onto the back of the bench.

"Have I got time? I have nothing but time. Right now, I am enjoying a wonderful stroll with Pooch. We are sitting in the park, just watching the world go by, and it's an absolutely beautiful morning. By the way, when are you coming to visit? It's about time, don't you think?" replied Channelize, teasingly.

"Oh, that sounds idyllic, Channelize," replied Amelia, enviously. "But you may be seeing me sooner than you think?" She paused, and then blurted out excitedly, "Yusef and I are getting married!" Channelize shrieked with joy.

"I don't believe he is finally going to marry you. I hope he knows what he's letting himself in for. When is the big day?"

Amelia told Channelize that they would officially get married in Morocco first, with all of Yusef's family present, and then she would have a blessing in England with her mother, Ruby, and other members of her family, in August, which was in one months' time. They spoke for a while about her plans, and her feelings regarding the religious aspects. Yusef hadn't insisted that Amelia become a Muslim, however, she had explained to him that it was something she might think about in the future.

"Obviously, if and when we have children, it may be an issue," she said to Channelize seriously. "But for now, it doesn't seem to be an issue for Yusef, or his family."

She had explained to Channelize that Yusef's family were not a traditional Moroccan family, and were very open-minded about Yusef's choice of partner. They discussed Channelize's life in France and Darius's work situation. Channelize had told Amelia about their friendship with Jake and Priscilla and finally, they talked about the new computer.

"How exciting, Channelize! I will give you my email address, it will be much cheaper to keep in touch that way. And, I can send you all the wedding photographs from Morocco! It will be just like old times, Channelize, we can do our 'ladies that lunch days' via the Internet," said Amelia, bursting with enthusiasm.

"Well, we can certainly try," replied Channelize. "Not that I am as confident as you are with technical gadgets, but I do need to learn more about it."

"Oh, once you get the hang of it, Channelize, you will be amazed at how much accessibility that you have. Have you spoken to Brook yet, on the web?" asked

Amelia confidently.

"No, not yet. I'm a bit nervous about using it at the moment. Darius is going to show me how to use things like that. He seems quite knowledgeable," Channelize said.

"Oh well, if Darius can figure it out, anyone can!" teased Amelia and they both burst into fits of laughter. It was just like old times.

Channelize walked home happily, thinking about Amelia and their conversation. She could hardly believe her best friend was getting married. She wasn't really surprised, as Amelia had been with Yusef for nearly four years and they hardly had a cross word between them.

Channelize and Darius would have to fly to England the last week of August for the wedding blessing. It would be an opportunity to visit Minnie and Herbert in their new apartment.

She was so excited to tell Darius all the events of the day, when he returned from work that evening.

Channelize spoke to Darius over dinner that night. He was happy to go to Amelia's wedding blessing, as he felt he deserved a break and some time off work. He was worn out, working with Jake most weekends and with Simon on the week days. He hadn't had much time to relax since they had arrived in France.

"I have something to tell you too, Channelize," he said, looking across the table at her, with a twinkle of mischief in his eyes. Channelize looked intrigued. He continued, "You know it's your birthday next week. Well, it's also someone else's too."

"Whose?" asked Channelize inquisitively.

"It's Priscilla's birthday too, on the same day!" he replied.

"Oh, how strange. All the time since I have known her, I never imagined her birthday was the same day as mine," Channelize said, intrigued.

"Well, Jake and I thought it would be nice to take you both out to dinner. Jake knows of a really lovely restaurant in the city centre. It's supposed to have the best French cuisine," said Darius.

"Is it expensive?" quizzed Channelize, coyly.

"I think so, but I am sure it is well worth it, according to Jake, anyway," Darius said, tucking into his pork chop.

"Oh. That's Okay, then," replied Channelize cheekily.

The rest of the evening and for the next few days, Darius and Channelize spent their time exploring and explaining the lap top. They had contacted Brook, and were now able to speak to him, live on webcam. Channelize was amazed, as Amelia had said she would be. She sent constant emails to Brook to keep up with his life and to share her thoughts and feelings. He would always email her straight away. She also kept up with the gossip with Amelia via email, too. Amelia would up-date her on all the gossip happening in Spain. She had told her that two distant friends of theirs had died in mysterious circumstances involving alcohol. Certain bars had closed down due to the recession, and finding work was ten times worse than it had ever been. Yusef, luckily, still had his job and she was hoping he would keep it for a while, at least until they got married, she had joked. Angelo's bar, apparently, was still slowly ticking over, not that she had been there much, since Channelize had left. But, according to Amelia, even Angelo had lost a good percentage of his trade due to the recession and the sterling exchange rate. It seemed the English, especially, couldn't afford to holiday in Spain. Amelia had heard rumours that Angelo was thinking of retiring in another year or so. She concluded, by saying that Yusef had seen Yanni. Apparently, during their conversation, Yanni had said that he was moving to France to try to find work. Apparently, he had friends living in Paris. Channelize was a little unnerved by this news. However, Paris was in the north of France and she was in the south, so it was a fair distance, she thought. She felt uneasy, just knowing that Yanni would be in the same country as herself and Darius — it was still, far too close for comfort. She decided not to ponder on it for too long and felt it best, not to mention it to Darius.

It was the eve of Channelize's birthday. Darius had bought her a beautiful, gold, key necklace which he said, was the key to his heart. He'd also invested in a bottle of her favourite perfume, 'The One' by Calvin Klein. She was over the moon, as she had secretly pined for that perfume for a while, but they could never afford it in the past. Brook had sent her a beautiful card with the skyline of New York City on the front. Inside it read, 'To a Special Mother, with love on her Birthday', from Brook, Georgia and Fabergé.'

Every year, Brook had always included his sister in his birthday cards for Channelize, and every year she would feel the same mixed emotions of happiness and sadness. She had lingered, reading the card over and over. A small tear had trickled from her cheek. The table was filled with cards she had received from Amelia, Judith, Minnie, her sister Toni, Priscilla and Jake, Simon and Penny and also a special card from Vivien.

She was dressed and ready to go to the restaurant. She wore a simple, black, knee-length dress, with her new gold necklace neatly placed on the outside of her dress. She tied her jet-black hair back in a knot, and wore delicate gold earrings. She carried with her, a red bag to match her red pump shoes. As she admired herself in the mirror, Channelize could not believe that she was the same women, less than three years ago. She looked elegant and sophisticated in her attire, nothing like the way she used to dress in Spain, where she wore the most outlandish clothing for attention, maybe, or to be rebellious. She wasn't quite sure, she thought. Her appearance would often shock the conservative 'clucking hens' as she would deliberately taunt them, with her bizarre dress sense. She wore the tiniest denim shorts, cut and torn, with small cropped tops, exposing her flat brown stomach. She wore the brightest and the loudest colours she could find. She had been self-destructive and extremely unhappy, then. All she wanted to do, was indirectly, stick two fingers up to the world. She had questioned herself many times, had she turned into an alcoholic, as her mother would often accuse her of being, similar to her aunt, Bella. But she had since come to realise that she was an unfortunate victim of her circumstances. It wasn't the drink that made her life… it was her life that made her drink. She had constantly had to fight her own corner, as Vivien would say. But now she had changed, she was in a much better place in her life. She felt loved and respected by a man, for the first time in years. Channelize lingered at the mirror, hardly recognising herself as she stood there. She looked mature and understated, the way the French ladies looked, dressed with an air of simplicity and refinement.

"All set then?" a voice said, as Darius poked his head around the doorway of the bedroom.

"Yes. Just coming, hun," replied Channelize. Just as he was about to disappear out of the door, Channelize shouted. "Darius, come here, hun, let's have a look at you." Darius appeared at the doorway, standing tall and proud. He was wearing a smart pair of dark trousers and a fitted red shirt, which caressed his muscular body. Channelize's body stirred with sexual desire. She had forgotten how handsome he could look. His hair was short, brown and neatly contoured. He was clean shaven and his facial skin, appeared tanned and glowing. She walked over to him and planted a penetrating kiss on his cherry lips. He seductively caressed his hands along her back and buttocks.

"You look beautiful, Channelize. My beautiful birthday girl," he said, and kissed her tenderly.

"You too, Darius. My handsome hunk!" she replied.

They left the apartment at eight o'clock. They were due to meet Jake and Priscilla at eight thirty. They found the Chevalier Restaurant quite easily. Jake had given Darius very easy directions. Darius ordered a Pastisse (which was a local drink in France, tasting similar to aniseed)for Channelize, and a glass of wine for himself, while they waited in the beautiful restaurant gardens for Jake and Priscilla, Darius explained to Channelize the history of the restaurant. Apparently, it had been used previously to stable horses. As Channelize looked around at the exquisite refurbishment, she found it very hard to believe that it was once dirty old stables, it was so lavish in its design. The only indications were the ceramic horse-head statues above the tables, leather saddles, and other equestrian memorabilia, conveniently placed around certain areas of the restaurant.

Jake and Priscilla appeared on the dot, at eight thirty. They greeted Channelize with a French kiss on both cheeks. Priscilla looked radiant in a patterned blue and cream chiffon dress and matching cream shoes,

Jake wore a pair of dark slacks and a silk, navy shirt.

"Happy birthday, Priscilla," Channelize said and Darius echoed.

"And to you, hen," replied Priscilla.

They ordered more drinks from the waiter and sat at a table, to study the menu.

Channelize had a chance to show off her French skills and explained to Darius, the dishes on display. Priscilla's French was much better though, as she had been visiting France for holidays for the past ten years, so she was automatically voted the best person to place the order. Jake's recommendation for Chevaliers was spot on, from their starter, right through to the dessert. The only way Channelize could best describe the food, was that it was the most tantalising, culinary experience she had ever enjoyed! The evening was relaxed and jovial. The Pastisse and wine flowed freely, while Channelize and Darius listened intently to the usual hilarious stories being told by Priscilla and Jake, accompanied by explosions of raucous laughter. It was the happiest birthday Channelize had experienced in a long time. Finally, two slightly intoxicated people stumbled out of the restaurant at closing time. The waiter had been hovering around the doorway, waiting to lock up. However, at the time they had been ignorant to the fact that the waiter had a home to go to, due to their childlike, drunken behaviour. But true to his impeccable French manners, he had been too polite to ask them to leave. Channelize commented on this as she linked arms with Priscilla, walking along the street.

"The French people are so polite, don't you think, Priscilla? she said with a drunken slur.

"Yeah... Very," replied Priscilla, looking at Channelize with a comical grin on her face

"They're just so polite and nice. Really, really nice," repeated Channelize, as she hung onto Priscilla for dear life. Priscilla stopped abruptly in the middle of the street and stared at Channelize in the eyes and blurted out, almost seriously,

"Yeah... Very!" They paused for a second, staring stupidly at each other and then Priscilla released an almighty roar of laughter and Channelize joined in. Darius and Jake were following behind. The pair had, very sensibly, not indulged in quite so much wine and Pastisse, as Priscilla and Channelize.

Jake shouted from behind them in his broad Scottish accent, "What are ya like? We can't take you two lassies, anywhere!

To which Priscilla turned around and shouted, "Oh... bugger off! And then burst into a melody of raucous laughter again, with which Channelize joined in. They behaved like two giggling schoolgirls, clinging on to each other and whispering childish comments about the two men behind. Finally, they reached Channelize's apartment. Jake peeled Priscilla's grip from Channelize's arm as they both tried to say their goodbyes. Channelize and Darius watched, amused, at Priscilla's comical antics as Jake tried desperately, to steer her along the street.

The next morning Channelize awoke to find the bed was empty. It suddenly dawned on her that Darius had gone to work, and that was the reason why he hadn't indulged in too much alcohol. She lay there, smiling to herself as she thought of the previous evening's events. Funnily enough, she felt great. She wasn't experiencing any sign of the banging headache or the normal, groggy lethargic feeling, which were her normal hangover symptoms. Maybe it was the Pastisse, she thought to herself. She hadn't drunk so excessively for ages, but it was her birthday, and it felt really refreshing to have a good laugh with great company. She liked Priscilla and Jake a lot, they were such a social and genuine couple. Priscilla worked from home for a pharmaceutical company and Jake worked hard on his project renovating the French house with Darius. Channelize envied Priscilla, in a way. At least she had a job and something she enjoyed doing all day long, and she got paid for it, which was an added bonus, in Channelize's book! She decided to get up. Pooch had been patiently waiting to go out for his walk. She showered and changed, grabbed some cereal and then took Pooch on his stroll through the park. When she returned, she began to tidy the kitchen. She wondered what had happened to all the drying up cloths. Puzzled, she searched underneath the kitchen sink.

"I bet Darius has used them for wiping his dirty hands on," she said to Pooch, rolling her eyes in disapproval. Channelize pulled open the clean laundry cupboard and searched for a cloth. She couldn't find one in there so she wandered around the apartment looking through drawers and cupboards. As she opened the wardrobe in the guest bedroom, she noticed a brown, cardboard box, as big as a shoe box, placed in the corner, on the floor. She slid it out and looked at the box, curiously. She grabbed a Stanley knife from the kitchen and proceeded to slice it open.

"Here they are!" she cried with relief, as the box revealed a pile of neatly packed drying cloths. 'This box must have been forgotten when we unpacked," she said to Pooch. She pulled out the cloth on the top and was about to close the box when she caught sight of something. It was brown and furry, stuffed into the bottom right-hand corner. At first, she was alarmed and quickly jumped away from the box, throwing it down onto the bed. She had thought the object was a mouse, or something horrible, lurking. Pooch looked startled too, and started to sniff wildly, inspecting the box. The object didn't move. She slowly and cautiously placed her hand inside the box and pulled out the furry ball. She straightened its fur and turned it around in her hand. Suddenly, she was aware of the little object. It had two dotted brown eyes, a dented nose, and quirky floppy ears. It was Bluebell.

Channelize's heart pulsed, the pain in her chest was almost unbearable. Her eyes widened as she gasped for breath. She had searched high and low for Bluebell whilst she had unpacked, she had thought he had been lost forever. She could only assume that Darius had put him in the box, and forgotten about him. Pooch sniffed and licked the little monkey's face. Channelize straightened Bluebell's nose, and stared hypnotically at the toy. It was smiling at her with its pencilled lips, smiling from ear to ear. She envisaged Fabergé's angelic face, looking up at her through Bluebell. She could hear Faberge's sweet-sounding voice saying,

"It's okay, Mummy. Don't be afraid. I'm happy now. Please don't blame yourself. I will always love you, Mummy... goodbye."

Channelize burst into tears and hugged the monkey to her face, squeezing it tightly with her finger tips. Her tears soaked up in Bluebell's fur. After half an hour, Channelize managed to compose herself. She walked slowly to the computer and sat Bluebell on the desk. His arms and legs dangled over the keyboard, his little face still smiling at her. Channelize forced a smile back. She sat, her eyes transfixed on the computer keys. She had thought about sending an email to Brook to tell him about the surreal experience she had just had. But as she placed her fingertips lightly onto the keyboard, she began to type, and without consciously thinking about it, she wrote these words.

Channelize was so excited to finally have the keys to her new apartment...

The End.